THE TERRORIST

CAROLINE B. COONEY

ISBN: 0-590-22853-6

Scheduled Pub. Date:
September 1997

Length:
208pp

Trim:
5$^1/_2$" x 8$^1/_4$"

Retail Price:
$15.95

Classification:
Middle Grade Fiction

Ages:
12 - up

Grades:
Junior High
& High School

LC: 96-42352

SCHOLASTIC PRESS
555 Broadway, New York, NY 10012

UNCORRECTED PROOFS

THE TERRORIST

THE
TERRORIST

BY

CAROLINE B. COONEY

Scholastic Press · New York

Library of Congress Cataloging-in-Publication Data

Caroline B. Cooney, 1948 –
The Terrorist / Caroline B. Cooney
p. cm.
Summary: Sixteen-year-old Laura, an American living in London, tries to find the
person responsible for the death of her younger brother Billy, who has been killed
by a terrorist bomb.

ISBN 0-590-22853-6
[1. Terrorism — Fiction. 2. London (England)— Fiction.
3. Mystery and detective stories— Fiction.] I. Title.

PZ7.C7834Te 1997
[Fic] — dc20   96-42352   CIP   AC

10 9 8 7 6 5 4 3 2 1

Printed in the U.S.A.
First printing, September 1997
The text type for this book was set in 12 point Janson Text.
Design by David Caplan

for London,
where Harold and Sayre and Louisa and I
lived for one marvelous year,
and for Nancy and Walt

THE TERRORIST

CHAPTER

1

At 6 a.m., Billy Williams began his paper route. He had had a paper route in Massachusetts, and a simple move to London, England, was not going to deprive him of his income. Billy kept a notebook in which he listed the differences between London and Boston. The first day of his route, he wrote, "They get up much later here." The following week, he added, "They don't tip much here."

Billy liked early morning London. It was darker and quieter than his little Boston suburb, where commuters and construction workers were eager to have coffee, read their newspaper, and get started on the day. In London, Billy felt mysterious and special at dawn. He loved misty mornings when his bike skidded wonderfully in the black slick of dying leaves that passed for autumn in England.

This morning, he paused at a bricklayer's job.

You could not go half a block in London without passing a brick wall being rebuilt. This country was mad for walls. There were no shortcuts across London yards. In England, bricks were stamped with the company's name. He had four different ones at home. Now he picked up a Walsham brick and stuck it in his book bag.

Billy finished delivering his papers, rode on home, and woke his mother. Then he tiptoed into his sleeping sister's room to turn the volume all the way up on her clock radio. It was pretty satisfying to hear Laura scream when the radio shocked her out of unconsciousness.

He fixed himself a bowl of Cheerios. When the family first arrived in London, they went crazy tasting everything different. But five months had passed. Now Billy yearned for the good old tastes of home.

Billy had a number of moneymaking activities going. When the Carlsons visited last month, they'd brought Billy an entire suitcase of real food. Now he was joyfully turning a big profit on Kraft macaroni and cheese and Oreo cookies.

Of course the embassy kids and the army kids could get that stuff through the commissary, but the rest of them, whose parents worked at Kodak or Xerox or Interface, would kill for American junk food. Yesterday, Molly Morgan bought a pack of Twinkies for four English pounds. It was two weeks' allowance, and everybody agreed it was worth it.

On another page in his notebook, Billy listed his profits in two currencies. The problem was, the dollar kept falling. At first, Billy had pictured a dollar that you lost hold of, and it fell to the ground. Slowly he figured out that a falling dollar was the one you still had, but it wasn't worth a dollar anymore. It was worth ninety cents, or eighty cents. It was not good to be living abroad when dollars were falling.

Billy was irked by London banks.

At home, First Federal made a big deal over deposits. He was earning interest on his $754 in Massachusetts. Here, they wouldn't even look at you. Literally. He'd never known such a place for ignoring a future millionaire. Billy had tried three banks, and nobody was interested in handling an eleven-year-old's account.

Billy decided that a new page was called for. In his terrible handwriting, he headed it:

BANKS I WILL NOT DO BUSINESS WITH WHEN I AM A MILLIONAIRE

Then he put four boxes of Kraft macaroni and cheese into his book bag.

His mother was making coffee and lowering slices of Danish bacon into the frying pan. She loved the grocery stores here. She was always trying a new puffy bakery loaf or another sort of bacon. Billy personally would shut down all those bakeries and sell Wonder bread. There was a real need in London for a cheap, spongy, white bread with ultrasoft crusts.

"What are you charging today?" said his mother.

"I'm getting two pounds each from Wendy, Spencer, and Megan, but Mary Alice is trading her best toilet paper."

His mother, who had spent the first ten of Billy's eleven years convincing him to use *any* toilet paper, was confused.

"For my collection," Billy told her, yet again. She never seemed on top of his collections, no matter how often he showed them to her. Billy sighed heavily and brought out a dark green three-ring notebook with clear plastic envelope pages. Neatly slotted within was his toilet paper. The British specialized in toilet paper with the texture of freezer wrap. "Mary Alice says she's got toilet paper with printing on it, Mom. Property of Camden Council. Do you think she's fibbing?" There would be no box of Kraft for Mary Alice if she were.

"I've drafted my letter, Mom," he added. "Can you type it for me?"

She took his soiled, mangled scrap of paper. Laboriously, he had printed out:

Dear Kraft,
I would like to be your London, England, distributor of Macaroni & Cheese. not the kind with the little can of cheese, nobody likes that. the small box with the blue top and the silver envlop of

yellow fake cheese. We will both make a big profit. and nobody but me has contacts all over London.

Sincerely; yours;
William Wardlaw Williams

His mother promised to type it for him. Billy gave her permission to correct punctuation but nothing else. His mother promised not to change a single word. "Airmail paper," he directed her. "I don't want to spring for an extra stamp."

He was halfway out the door before he registered his mother's mild voice calling after him. "Schoolbooks?" she suggested.

Billy frowned. "Oh yeah." It annoyed him that school included school. He loved school. He especially loved London International Academy, because you had to take the tube (the subway) to get there, but it was too bad that school meant classes as well.

Billy stuffed two out of the possible five texts into his book bag, trusting that somebody in the class would be willing to share with him, especially when he still had half a bag of M&M's left. He dashed up the sidewalk, high brick walls on his right hiding the front gardens of Victorian row houses, and parked cars guarding his left. Londoners were excellent drivers. They could parallel park anywhere along their skinny little roads. Billy loved the bus and truck drivers who, without slowing down, could fit like bread in a toaster down the narrow alleys.

He passed a row of Minis. He loved those cars. They were so tiny, you always thought you could just put a strap around their middles and use them for suitcases. He raced past the church where his mother had expected to meet the kind of people she read about in British mystery novels: avid gardeners, retired mayors, and handsome barristers. It turned out, however, that nobody in London went to church but the Episcopal priests. This raised the English greatly in Billy's opinion. When he got home, he would recommend it to their minister as a timesaving device.

Once he reached the Underground station, Billy said "Hi" to the flower man, who was Asian, and "Good Morning" to the newsstand man, who was Pakistani, and "How are ya?" to the ticket woman, who was Jamaican. "Cheers," they said to him, and when he bought something, "Ta, luv." Billy loved how they said "Thank you" in Brit-speak.

He inspected all posters and signs to see if any were sagging enough that he could legitimately remove them on the grounds that they were a danger to passersby. He had collected a Journey Planner (the complete London Underground map), a pink flamingo poster advertising the Zoo, and his very favorite:

If Your Personal Stereo Bothers the
Other Passengers, You Are Contravening
The Bye Laws.

Whenever his mother really riled him, Billy liked to tell her she was contravening his bye laws.

The poster he yearned for most was the Jubilee Line map, his personal tube line. It was better than anybody else's. Robbie, for example, had to take the Metropolitan, a sleazy, slow, crowded line. However, the Jubilee Line sign was firmly attached.

He decided against spending his hard-earned money on Polo candy, checked vending machines for abandoned change, and ambushed Chris and Georgie as they joined him on the platform. The boys placed bets on how soon their train would arrive. Chris had a stopwatch. Billy won and got five pence each off Chris and Georgie.

"What're you going to do with all that money, anyhow?" said Chris. "You never spend it."

"Going to China," said Billy. He patted an embroidered badge on his jeans jacket, a map of China his mother had obediently sewn on.

"No, really," said Chris.

"Yes, really. A year ago I decided I'm going to see every inch of China."

The boys considered the size of China. Every inch sounded like a lot.

Once on the train, none of them sat. It would be unthinkable to take a seat when you could stand by the doors, swaying, feet spread, refusing to hold a metal post and too short to reach a hanging strap. Billy prided himself on never having fallen into anybody.

He gazed with superiority at the businessmen and women whose briefcases were hugged between their knees. Leather cases always made him think of his family's arrival at Heathrow Airport. Signs everywhere said not to leave baggage unattended. "Are they worried somebody would steal my pajamas?" Billy had asked his father.

"No, they're worried about bombs," explained his father. "Terrorists."

Billy's mother was so horrified by that, she reacted like a shepherd whose flock is surrounded by wolves. Constantly watching their dozen suitcases and tugging to make the pile more compact, she eyed innocent strangers for signs of evil intent.

Billy yearned to abandon a suitcase and see what happened next. Either Scotland Yard or MI 5 would seize it, which would be worth the whole flight, or else a terrorist would steal it and Billy could seize the terrorist, which would be worth any two flights.

Annoyingly, his parents had refused to leave a suitcase.

The train pulled into Baker Street, where they would change lines. The three boys hurled themselves out into the belowground corridors and sets of stairs. A train was waiting, doors open, car packed. They crammed themselves in. No need to hang on to anything this time: other bodies would keep them upright.

At the third stop, they leaped from the car, and began the race to see who would get outside to the fresh air first. It was another five pence for the winner. Billy firmly believed that pennies added up, even British pennies.

But he got caught by passengers swarming onto the train, so Chris and Georgie got way ahead. Chris yelled triumphantly over his shoulder, "I'm gonna win this time!"

Billy sprinted after them, slithering among the Indians, Asians, and Africans who made up the English population that he had thought would look like Robin Hood and Maid Marian.

Passengers funneled toward the only working escalator. Tired people stood on the right side, clutching briefcases, handbags, and shopping trolleys, little wire suitcases on wheels that Londoners used to bring their groceries home. Energetic people ran up the left edge as the steps moved under their feet.

Chris and Georgie were almost out of sight.

Billy tried to elbow past some old ladies, but somebody caught his arm. Expecting to be yelled at, Billy prepared to hide his American accent. Billy didn't mind being yelled at, but he hated it when somebody inevitably muttered, "Oh, those rowdy American children!"

If there was one thing English children were not, it was rowdy. Sometimes Billy wondered if they were even alive.

Actually at London International Academy, he was in classes with every nationality *except* the English.

They had their own schools to go to. He was living right here in England and had tons of friends and none of them were English.

Billy decided on another new page in his notebook. He'd have a Nationality List. A Country Collection. Just in his sixth-grade homeroom were kids from Denmark, Iran, Syria, Argentina, Israel, Hong Kong, and America. He was pretty sure Juan was from somewhere else entirely, and Priya might be from India.

But the man who caught his arm actually smiled, saying, "Your friend dropped this."

Billy was amazed and pleased by this unusual helpfulness. "Oh gee, thanks a lot," he said. He grabbed the package and tore up the escalator.

Stopped by a woman who was awkwardly balancing a stroller with a baby across the width of the rising stairs, he glanced down at the package.

Funny.

He didn't remember Georgie or Chris carrying anything. Just book bags slung on their shoulders.

There was something very British about the package.

Not American.

The whole way it was wrapped. The cheapness of the cellophane tape. The texture of the brown paper.

He remembered the signs and warnings at Heathrow. Do Not Leave Any Luggage Unattended. He remembered the fire drills at school, which the big kids said were really bomb drills.

There was a sickening moment of knowledge.

He could not throw the package into the innocent crowd.

There was no place to set it down.

Nor could he give it back.

In front of him was a sleeping baby.

Oh, Mom! thought Billy, turning away from the stroller and wrapping himself around the package.

The package exploded.

CHAPTER 2

Laura Williams took the city bus. Buses were slower than the Underground, but she met more of her friends. Plus the air was better.

Laura loved her monthly commutation ticket and the flair with which she used both bus and Underground. She cherished her knowledge of complex routes. That was true urban sophistication.

Laura stood on Finchley Road, reveling in the wind that lifted her hair and turned her skirt into a flaring tulip. Wind was so romantic. Laura waited for the 113 bus and Eddie's big, crazy wave.

Of course, nobody was as crazy as her brother, Billy.

Laura was proud of Billy, but only when nobody knew she was related to him. In public, Billy was embarrassing, and a person got tired of being embarrassed. Like the time Billy talked Mom into buying him a purple punk wig, which he wore to school with a necklace of bicycle chains. Or the many times he went to school in a suit of Dad's, pant legs rolled up six times, sleeves shoved up past his elbows, swinging his book bag like a lion trainer's chair. Plus of course the toilet paper collection and the profiteering on macaroni.

Eddie thought of himself as an exciting, disruptive kind of guy, but he was nothing compared to Laura's brother, Billy.

Right now, Laura had two concerns in life.

The first was the Junior-Senior Thanksgiving dance. She did not have a date.

Oh sure, Eddie would take her, but he was an everyday friend. Laura wanted somebody dark and handsome and mysterious and romantic. Once Laura asked Jehran to bring forth a terrific brother or cousin who would fit this need. Jehran was amused by the thought that any brother or cousin of hers would want to associate with an American girl. Jehran was from Iran, or Iraq, or one of those places, but had never lived there, as her father had been a friend to the wrong people, and they had had to flee when the other guys came to power. (Actually they had fled *before* that, which was the whole trick to fleeing: you had to know when to get out.) Jehran's family had tried life in Buenos Aires, and Paris, and now London, in search of a happy exile.

As for Eddie, his real name was Erdam Yafi, and he, like Jehran, was from almost everywhere. His family was fabulously wealthy and lived way out of London in an actual palace. (Laura had been there, and was very disappointed. Palaces in England did not have turrets and moats; they were immense grim stone houses with several million windows across the front. The palace in Disney World was better.) Sometimes his father's driver brought Eddie to school, but more often Eddie liked to be driven to a bus stop so he could get on a bus with other kids.

Eddie wore the oldest, most torn blue jeans in the Academy. His American accent was Texan, from the year he'd been in Houston. Eddie wanted to be with Laura every minute of the day because he loved her hair. He was always trying to touch her hair, which was deep gold and straight as ribbons. Laura would hit his hand away, yelling, "Eddie! Leave my hair alone!"

Eddie was always asking if they could go out to a pub. Laura's mother was beginning to say yes to things like that, as long as it was a group and not a date. Laura, for the last two Fridays, had had the unbelievable, completely not-American delight of going to a pub. The boys ordered beer, and Laura stuck to Coke so her mother wouldn't kill her. The other girl to go along was Consuela.

Con's father was with the American Embassy. They were originally from New Jersey, but hadn't even visited in years. They'd lived in Singapore, Cairo, and London instead. Mr. Vikary had plans for his daughter Con to make a mark in the world.

All Laura's friends studied.

Laura had never met such a studying crowd.

Not only did they study intensively, they talked about their class assignments, grades, and college goals instead of gossip or dates or basketball games or anything genuinely interesting.

Laura knew college was out there somewhere, like dessert after dinner, but she was too busy telephoning friends, planning her wardrobe, and thinking about the weekend to consider college just yet.

Con intended to go to Yale or Princeton and was very concerned with her Extracurricular Activities. She had an immense, appalling list of Extracurricular Activities and she was always in charge of each of them.

Laura had never participated in an Extracurricular Activity and certainly didn't want to start now, what with the Thanksgiving dance coming up.

It was something Laura could not understand. How did people like Con get all this done, anyhow? How did they get a ninety-eight average in trigonometry, and an A plus on their European history term paper, and a Perfect in their Shakespeare tragedy essay, and still be in Student United Nations, the English-American Committee for Better Understanding, the Jazz Band, the Concert Choir, *three* sports, and never miss a meeting of the London Walk Club?

The London Walk Club killed Laura.

These kids would meet one afternoon a week and

walk someplace. Perhaps it would be a Super Tour of Westminster Abbey. Or a hike to the British Museum to gaze upon the Rosetta Stone.

Every now and then, Laura went along because her friends did, and because Con insisted this would look good on college applications. Colleges, she said, liked to know you were interested in everything from Shakespeare to Inner-city Problems Abroad.

Laura was not interested.

Laura was interested in a date.

She was, however, beginning to worry about her own college application. On that blank white page where Con would list 207 Extracurricular Activities, what was Laura going to list? Phone calls. Fashion. Yelling at her little brother. Making brownies.

Actually, you would have to strike making brownies. It was not possible to bake brownies in England, as neither the ingredients nor the right oven existed, and furthermore Laura had to have a Duncan Hines or a Betty Crocker mix.

Luckily, for friendship, Con had normal human moments and Con, too, wanted a dark, handsome, romantic date for the dance.

Laura often thought that when her brother, Billy, grew up, he was going to be the heartthrob of his entire school. You could see in his arms the muscles that were going to come. And his thick, dark hair, which he never combed or brushed after a shower (assuming you could shove him into a shower with the water on in the first place), was going to lie around on his forehead, and girls would want to sweep it away from his flirty eyes.

However, Billy had a long way to go.

He had to get out of sixth and finish up seventh and eighth, which anybody knew were the worst years of all humanity. Signs of real life would sprout during ninth, and finally in tenth grade Billy would be a person. By then, Laura would be away at college.

Still waiting for the 113 (buses with a dozen different routes had come on time, but the 113 had chosen to be late), Laura considered college forms.

Her only true hobby was grading boys and men.

Most boys in school Laura considered to be Six or Seven. For some reason, it was hard to give out an Eight or Nine. You went straight to Ten. There were several Tens at whom Laura often gazed with adoration.

Dear College: My hobby is Not Going to Cultural Events or Places of Architectural Note. So far, I have not gone to Westminster Abbey and I also have not gone to Windsor Castle. Just last week I did not go to Canterbury Cathedral. I have not gone to the required Shakespeare performances, but have sold my tickets and bought clothes instead.

Somehow Laura had a feeling that colleges, like her mother and father, would think she should take advantage of a London year instead of throwing it away.

Laura loved London. She was from a small suburb and, like everybody else in America, considered a car the only way to move, and she was correct: at home, public transportation was a trial and a joke. But in

London she could hop on a bus, take the tube, or flag down a taxi. From Shakespeare to sweatshirt shopping, she was free the way no kids at home were until they had their own car.

The 113 appeared with Eddie waving insanely.

She got on, said "Hi" to Eddie and three other L.I.A. students, and the five of them sorted out with whom they would have lunch, whether anybody was going on the London Walk that afternoon, and had Laura heard about the escaped terrorists?

At L.I.A., they had bomb practice, the way in Massachusetts they had fire drills. L.I.A. students marched out the door and lined up on the sidewalk while London police timed them and teachers checked lockers and possible bomb-hiding spots. Everybody was happy, especially the people who got out of math.

London International Academy was very security-minded.

Several kids arrived at school in their own limousines with their own guards. There were two kids in the Lower School who were not allowed to play at anybody's house after school because their parents were worried they might become kidnap victims. Lots of kids didn't have their phone number listed in the school directory. You had to telephone their embassy. You'd leave a message, the embassy personnel would be the ones who actually called your friend up, and finally your friend would call back.

Laura loved that.

That was so romantic.

She wanted to date a boy who didn't have a phone number in the directory. A boy who was fabulously wealthy, living in a house with his own submachine-gun-carrying guards on the ground floor, pacing back and forth to keep out the terrorists.

Like Michael. Michael would be perfect. He possessed all of the above and, furthermore, was a Ten. However, Michael had thoughtlessly begun dating Kyrene.

"No, I didn't hear anything," said Laura. "What terrorists?" She wondered how the embassies would handle privacy once *Caller I.D.* appeared in London.

The five teenagers changed buses. They were disgusted with Laura. Hadn't she watched the morning news? Hadn't she read the morning paper?

They were exceedingly news-conscious, these kids. Their parents worked in the embassy or were in the army or had an overseas assignment from their corporation. Changes in the world meant changes in their parents' jobs and the kids' lives, sometimes overnight. And yet, as much as they could, L.I.A. students kept their own news hidden. Lots of times, kids didn't even want to say what country they were from.

Like, if Laura was sitting at lunch with a boy from Syria (Syria hated Israel) and also with a boy from Israel (Israel hated Syria) and then up came another dark-complexioned kid (not the sallow dark of India, but warm, Middle Eastern dark) whose country Laura didn't know—well, the school rule was, *Don't Ask*.

Laura and Billy had learned right away that they must not discuss countries of origin. It didn't do. These kids' fathers were probably at war with each other, or selling each other weapons, or telling lies prior to signing a peace treaty, or denying each other billion-dollar loans.

It especially didn't do for Laura, who could never remember which country was which, anyway. She could not tell Iran from Iraq. It was unfair that they had such similar names. How were you supposed to get a grip on them when they were only one letter different? Jehran had said twenty times whether her people were from Iran or Iraq, and still Laura forgot.

That made her the only junior at L.I.A. who did. The rest knew exactly the status of peace talks in the Arab world, and exactly who in Africa was having a civil war, and exactly who in South America now had a decent economy.

But Laura had learned an important lesson. Other people so enjoyed giving *their* opinions that they liked her even better if she had *no* opinion. Then they could educate her to their way of thinking.

Laura nodded agreeably when Arabs told her how awful Israel was, and then nodded agreeably when Israelis told her how awful Arabs were. The world was a simple place, Laura had decided. The key was not to get worked up over things.

The bus halted with a lurch at their stop, which was in front of the tube exit and a mere three-block walk to L.I.A.

Laura was thinking that maybe terrific blond Andrew (a Ten) would talk to her after history. Maybe in the cafeteria she'd finally be in line next to that splendid hunk Mohammed (as opposed to Muhamet, who was sleazy, and Mohammet, who dated Jenny), and then—

Ambulances and fire trucks filled the sidewalks.

People were screaming and sobbing.

Police and teachers from L.I.A. were rushing back and forth.

Her friends—Andrew, Con, Mohammed, Jehran, Bethany—were clinging to one another.

What had happened? Who was hurt? It must be very bad, it must be somebody from school, it must be—

Laura's clothing shivered on top of her skin.

Billy took the Underground.

Billy could be such a jerk. He liked to play with the car doors. He'd stick his head out, or his foot, and yank himself back in the nick of time. Laura was always yelling at him.

But of course it couldn't be Billy, because Billy was the kind of person who survived. Billy would always land on his feet.

Andrew saw Laura first, and turned toward her, his eyes bright and shocked.

Jehran tugged a policeman's arm, and pointed at Laura.

Mohammed and Con and Bethany shifted to face in Laura's direction. Her math teacher looked up and stared at her.

It seemed to Laura that all those people swung toward her, as if attached in a chorus line. As if her own foot, leaving the bus, landing on the pavement, signaled them.

She let go of her book bag. She held up her palm to stop bad news as if it were traffic.

Beneath her, London swayed: a tube train passed below her feet like an aftershock.

"No," said Laura Williams, trying to get back on the bus. Trying to go back in time. "No. Not Billy."

CHAPTER

3

Laura had been crying so much, her face was as swollen as if she'd walked into a beehive. Her eyes were nearly puffed shut, and her fair complexion was mottled and patchy.

It was Laura who had been talking to the police; Laura who had been phoning everywhere for her father, and not found him.

I'm sixteen, thought Laura. In America, I lived in a little white house with a picket fence and maple trees. I lived in the same town where Louisa May Alcott grew up. I've never had a drink except Coca-Cola. I've never tried a cigarette. I'm ordinary. I'm the most ordinary American there is. And my very own brother has just been killed by terrorists.

Billy had forgotten to take his lunch. It rested on the kitchen counter in the Williamses' flat. The peanut butter and grape jelly sandwich was in its plastic bag, cut into triangles and not squares, the way Billy required. It was made of the only peanut butter Billy would eat: crunchy Jif, mailed by Grandma every month. Welch's grape jelly was mailed in the same package, because if you asked for grape jelly in England, they looked at you as if you wanted jelly made from locusts or pizza. They would tempt you with their designer marmalade and their strawberry jam with Cointreau, but Billy wanted only Welch's grape jelly with the cartoon glass.

He would never eat that lunch.

He would never finish up the grape jelly so he could drink from the Tom and Jerry glass.

The flat was full of people. A horde of Englishmen filled her home. Laura's mother had come back from her volunteer morning at the Royal Free Hospital and found them there: Laura and the police.

But no Billy.

Never again Billy.

Her mother's pixie face was twisted like paper crushed in your hand to throw in the trash. "I want to see my son," she said over and over.

They said it would be better not to see Billy. There wasn't much to see. Just bits and pieces.

Laura wanted to scream. She could even hear her scream, the huge ripping violence of her own noise, but she did not scream. She wanted to pick up candlesticks and library books and cans of tomato sauce and throw them at these intruders. But she sat quietly with her arm around her mother.

"Who are all these people?" asked her mother. Her mother had become dim, like a bulb going out. They kept covering the same topics, but it didn't stick and shortly, Mom would ask again.

"Everybody," Laura said. "Scotland Yard, Scotland Yard's antiterrorist squad, the Metropolitan Police, representatives from the American Embassy, and faculty from the school."

Her mother said, "Please leave my flat." She even remembered to say "flat" and not "apartment." But nobody left.

"Laura, where is Daddy?" said her mother. And to the strangers, "Where is my husband? Where did he go? Why isn't he here?" And to herself, "Thomas? Thomas?" as if he were hidden by the Englishmen pacing in her living room.

"We can't find him, Mom. He's on the road somewhere."

Dad might not get home till six, or seven, or even eight. Laura looked at her watch. Her father had gotten her the watch as a moving-to-London present. Bribe, actually, to make her cooperate. Laura had not wanted to come. "Miss my junior year?" she had shrieked back there in Massachusetts. "Leave my friends? Never! I won't! You can't do this to me!"

The watch had tiny setting moons and suns that rotated around the clock face, like signposts to an antique world.

If I had thrown enough tantrums, she thought,

maybe we would have stayed in Massachusetts, and Billy would still be alive.

It ticked like a bomb inside her heart: *we didn't have to come.*

"Don't put it over the radio," her mother begged the police for the tenth time. "Thomas listens to the radio when he drives. You can't let him hear it over the radio."

They promised that Billy's name would not be broadcast, but the news of an American child's death had been on the air since ten o'clock that morning.

Daddy's going to hear it, thought Laura dully. *Eleven-year-old boy from London International Academy killed by package bomb.* He'll hear it and he'll say to himself, *Don't worry, it can't be my son.* And he'll drive a little farther, and he'll be furious with himself for not taking the cellular phone on this trip—he left it accidentally in Darlington; they've got it right there—and he'll stop to use a public phone, and he'll say to Mom, all casual, *"Nicole, honey? Um . . . Billy have a good day?"* He'll be holding his breath, but he won't make a big deal of it, because it can't be Billy.

It's Billy.

"Laura, we have a policewoman to sit with your mother for a moment. Would you find us a photograph of your brother, please?"

The photograph albums had been left in America. They were wrapped in an old sheet and tucked carefully in Grandma's attic. But school pictures had just been done at L.I.A. Laura brought an uncut sheet to the police.

Billy was handsome. Dark floppy hair over a smooth, tan face, much darker in complexion than anybody else in the family. His easy wide American grin showed perfect white American teeth that were not going to need braces. For his school portrait, he'd worn a white sweatshirt with the school logo: a map of the world—scarlet land on blue seas. Behind Billy, the sky was as blue and clear as Arizona, which puzzled the police; London did not have skies like that. "It's a backdrop," said Laura. "They always use that fake sky backdrop for school pictures."

Back home, like millions of American households, the Williamses had had an entire wall of school pictures with the same gaudy fake blue sky. Laura and Billy in kindergarten, first, second, and so on. "You pay fifteen ninety-five for a pack," said Laura, "because you want to trade the little wallet pictures. But nobody ever really does and by spring you've lost them all, anyway."

They cut apart the wallet-sized pictures and passed them out among each other.

What a kick Billy would have gotten out of it. Scotland Yard studying his photo.

"Talk to me about Billy," said one man. He was wearing a too-large wool suit, as if he had recently lost weight, but not enough to warrant buying a new suit. Laura had dimmed like her mother; she could not seem to get their names, even though Laura was terrific with names.

"We need to find out if Billy was a specific choice," the policeman went on. "He was murdered the day after terrorists escaped from their courtroom. He might have seen something."

At L.I.A. you were required to take current events no matter what other history class you might also have, because these particular students were so often caught in the maelstrom of changing governments.

"London simmers," her current events teacher liked to say. Mr. Hollober was Canadian. Laura loved his pale accent. "Exiles fill this city, and they're all in a bad mood. All mad at somebody. Iraqi, Tamil, Nigerian, Cypriot, Azerbaijani, Hong Kong Chinese, Irish, Israeli, Palestinian, Kenyan."

It made Laura dizzy to think of so many countries sitting here in London, riding the tube and mad at each other. Or mad at America. There were an awful lot of people out there who didn't think much of America. Laura was still trying to get used to that since as far as she knew, America was perfect, and she was luckier than they would ever be because she was American.

"London," Mr. Hollober would say, "is the seismograph of the world. A needle that shakes at the slightest political tremor."

Had Billy touched the needle? Or the people who held it?

"Or," said the policeman, "the bomb might have nothing to do with the escapees. Some other terrorist group might have done it. Nobody has claimed responsibility yet, so we have nothing to go on. Finally, Billy might have been chosen specifically as a child, or specifically as an American child."

Laura could hardly think about who had killed Billy. It filled her mind too much, knowing that Billy was dead. We need Daddy, she thought. We need him right now.

Her father had been sent to England to close down factories. His company made electronic components, but business was poor and they were ending European operations. Daddy hated being the bad guy, but to be the American bad guy in towns already deeply depressed and jobless—well, it was not Laura who was sorry they had come. It was Dad. Laura had fallen in love with London and with L.I.A., Billy loved everything, anyhow, and Mom was having the adventure of her life. Dad had said only a few weeks ago that he couldn't last much longer. "You have to last through the school year!" Laura had said. "You can't ruin my junior year! What about my friends?" They had had a good laugh.

But if they had decided to go home last week, Billy would still be alive.

She told the police about Billy.

She brought them his notebook. She hated letting them touch it. What if they laughed at Billy? She showed them his brick collection. She didn't even want them to touch the bricks. What if they didn't understand? What if they couldn't tell that Billy was the most interesting person on earth?

But he was not on earth now.

She tried to tell herself that Billy was up in heaven, whipping it into shape, investigating the corners, selling stuff to naive angels.

A lump the size of a football lay in Laura's throat. It blocked not only speech, but also action and thought. Billy, who jumped into life like an Olympic champion. Feet first. Never scared, never flinching, never worried.

"Why couldn't it have been me?" she cried out. "I want to be the one instead. I want the package in *my* hands. I want it to blow *my* ribs apart and paste *my* brains on the wall and spray *my* blood on the baby carriage!"

The man in the too-large jacket put his arms around Laura, the way her father would have, if only they could find her father. "The baby lived, Laura," he said. "Witnesses thought that Billy knew, that he tried to protect the baby. The baby isn't even badly hurt. The mother will lose her leg, but not her life. She'll still bring her baby up."

"We don't get to bring Billy up, though!"

Nobody said anything to that.

"And all those witnesses," she said, feeling her way

toward knowledge. "They must have seen who did it. What did they tell you—all those witnesses?"

"They were witnesses to Billy's death," said the policeman, "but not to the moment in which Billy was handed the bomb. Nobody saw that. Trains continued to leave the station, and commuters continued to leave the Underground. The killer, or killers, left easily and without being known."

The killer.

Somebody chose my brother, thought Laura. Somebody looked at my brother Billy and picked him to die.

Laura's body switched channels. She moved from tears to wrath, from dim to volcanic.

I'm going to find them, she thought, and her body burned with the fever of revenge. A flush of rage crept over her, and shook her, so that her teeth actually chattered with hate and her cheeks actually darkened with intent.

I'm going to kill them. She felt in her hands the ability to hold a weapon; the ability to use it; and the need.

They're going to die just the way Billy did.

"When will somebody claim responsibility?" Laura demanded.

The policeman looked tired. "Usually, if they do, it's quick. Several hours have passed, though. Maybe nobody will admit it. Maybe some group that had nothing to do with it will claim to have done it, just for publicity. Bomb analysts will try to learn who did it by comparing Billy's bomb to previous bombs."

"Why do the terrorists tell the police anything?" said Laura. "I would think they'd want to keep it a secret."

He shook his head. "The point is to terrify. To show off power. To prove they can do whatever they want and hurt whoever they want whenever they want to do it. The only silver lining to terrorism is that they give you the first clue."

Outside, it was already getting dark. London was so far north. You didn't know that, living in America. You thought it was sort of across the Atlantic from New York. But it wasn't. It was across from Labrador. You got sun-starved here.

The policewoman coaxed Laura's mother to go lie down in her bedroom.

Laura walked over to the front window. Every flat on Heathfold Gardens had white curtains covering the windows: gauzy, or lacy, polyester or cotton, nobody kept bare glass. Laura's mother had found it claustrophobic, and took her curtains down, which meant you could spot the Williamses' flat blocks away. It was the only one without that extra barricade for privacy.

The English loved privacy. They didn't let people into their gardens very easily, never mind their hearts. They pronounced it *prih*-vissy, which sounded even more private.

Americans were not awfully good at privacy. Especially Billy.

Had he invaded somebody's privacy? Somebody who really, really had reason to care?

In the street below, people in gossipy bunches stared or talked or held television cameras, hoping to invade the privacy of the Williams family.

"Stand clear of the windows, Miss Williams," said the policeman gently.

"Why?"

"We don't know the purpose of Billy's death. Maybe it's your family the bombers want."

"My *family?*" Laura thought suddenly of her father, ending the income of a hundred workers. Maybe they couldn't reach Daddy because Daddy wasn't all right either! *Maybe there had been two bombs.*

She tried to tell the policeman this, but she couldn't stick the words in order. She couldn't get the syllables lined up right. A queer jumble fell out of her mouth, as if she were attempting a foreign language.

Terrorism had worked.

She was terrified.

CHAPTER

4

Thomas Williams enjoyed standing in the queue. He liked the word "queue," with its vowels lined up. It amused him that he, Thomas Williams, had learned to get in line like a good little boy and wait his turn, even if it meant standing outside in the rain.

He had all the family's passports with him.

Originally they had had one passport for the four of them, but Billy objected to this, insisting he needed his own. Billy loved his passport: the small dark blue folder with the golden eagle and the photograph of himself: the proof for all the world that he, William Wardlaw Williams, was born in the USA.

Laura had reacted like a teenage girl, appalled by her picture, afraid the customs officials might actually think that hideous girl with the bad hair was her.

Thomas grinned, thinking of family. Nicole, Laura, and Billy were all he had to smile about these days.

Thomas Williams was desperate to take a break from England and the nightmare of his job.

Such a tiny country. Literally a drive-through. He needed to stretch. He was just too close to everything here; there was no escape. In this miniature country, everything was in your own backyard. His wife, Nicole, wanted to go back to the States for Christmas vacation (this was how the English referred to America—"the States"; whereas Americans never thought of their country as "the States," which made it sound like fifty places, they thought of it as one—America), but Thomas knew if they went home now, when work was so awful, he could never force himself to return.

So he was at the Russian Embassy, getting visas for a Christmas trip to Russia. He had never cared about travel, but London changed this. Now he was enthralled by the world. He couldn't wait to take Billy to St. Petersburg and Moscow. The thing with a son like Billy—although you could never take your eyes off the kid, because Billy was neither sensible nor careful—was that he was so rewarding. Billy was so much fun to take anywhere.

Christmas in Russia. Billy would love it.

Laura would want to know why they couldn't stay in London like civilized people.

Nicole would giggle and clap. Thomas loved a woman who was forty and still said, "Ooooo, cool, neat, when do we leave?"

It had taken all afternoon to get the visas. Thomas was delighted with the surprise of it: handing out the passports at dinner and asking everybody what they found inside.

He could hardly wait till Billy figured out that his passport now contained the official stamp from the Russian Embassy. Billy would go wild. *Russia!* he'd yell. *Way to go, Dad!*

So Thomas Williams was laughing to himself as he began the long, slow drive through London traffic. No matter how bad London traffic was, and no matter that he still felt the occasional jolt of worry driving on the left, it was never half so bad as Boston, where tourists were regularly found trembling by the side of the road, no longer caring where Paul Revere's house was, wanting only to leave Boston behind forever, preferably with somebody else driving.

Behind him, a tiny police car signaled him to pull over. How do grown men fold up small enough to fit behind the wheel of that miniature car? Thomas wondered.

He was unable to think of a traffic rule he had broken. Running his mind over his driving, he rolled down his window. "Hi there," he said to the policeman.

The young officer, who leaned down to the car window, was very grim. "Mr. Thomas Williams?"

How could he know my name? Thomas thought, surprised, and then, in the carefully controlled expression on that young face, he saw something. He felt the stab in his heart that all parents feel when something goes wrong fast. He couldn't speak. He fumbled, his hand trying to speak for him, plucking at the officer's jacket. *My children?*

"My children?" he whispered.

The police wanted to question Chris and Georgie, who had been on the tube train with Billy.

But they couldn't talk to Chris. His father was with the American Embassy. The moment Chris's dad found out what had happened, he was at the school like a shot, collecting Chris and putting him on the next plane to his aunt in Denver.

Chris was airborne before Mr. Williams even knew that Billy was dead. Chris didn't have time to pack anything but clothes. Not his skateboard, not his baseball mitt, not his personal stereo with which he loved to contravene the bye laws.

"You could have waited till we interviewed Chris," said the police to Chris's father.

Chris's father shook his head. "He didn't see a thing. He was out of the station by the time it happened. All that matters to me is Chris being safe. If somebody is after the kids at London International Academy, he's not going to find my kid."

o   o   o

Billy's collections were extensive.

Flattened candy wrappers from new and different English candy bars.

Free Australian magazines.

Dozens of train and travel tickets jammed down into a big glass jar.

Beer coasters his father had saved from pubs.

Newspapers in foreign languages: Arabic and Finnish and German and Italian.

The police took the newspapers seriously: what had this little American boy been doing with Arab newspapers?

There were several piles of Irish newspapers, with heavy coverage of freedom fighters. Mr. Evans called them terrorists.

"We're part Irish," said Laura. "Billy felt he was collecting his history."

"Tell me about that," said Mr. Evans.

"It doesn't mean anything. We just are." Laura thought of herself as American, and had to dredge up the knowledge that way back there in her family were the original countries. She didn't like Mr. Evans's concern with the Irish newspapers. It was just a collection. Before she moved here, Laura would have said the English and Irish were cousins, but these cousins, it turned out, had fought on and off for generations in Northern Ireland. Just when you thought there would be peace, somebody shot somebody again, and there wasn't.

"The escaped terrorists," said Mr. Evans, "were Irish. But I have just learned that they have been picked up. Nowhere near London. It seems quite impossible they could have had anything to do with Billy. But I still wonder why he collected these newspapers."

Laura shrugged. Some people were collectors and some people were not. She thought of the escaped terrorists. *Picked up.* How had that happened? How did you spot a terrorist and pick him up?

"Laura, I need you to tell me everything, from A to Zed."

Zed.

Billy, of course, had adopted every possible British phrase. He, too, closed the alphabet with zed, not zee. He used the loo, not the bathroom. He would never have permitted a turnip to enter his mouth, but he always wanted his mother to buy some so he could claim to have eaten swedes for dinner. He wrote with a Biro instead of a Bic, and eagerly put plasters on his cuts instead of Band-Aids.

Once he heard a London mother refer to her little boy's sneakers as "plimsolls." He loved this word, and often used his British-est voice to say, "I'll just plimsoll on down to the corner and buy myself some Polos."

"You can't plimsoll," his mother said. "It's not a verb."

"It is now," Billy said. "I've Americanized it."

Laura stood in the stranger-jammed flat as if she were all alone. As if she had lost everything in life that mattered. Her brother, Billy, was never going to plimsoll anywhere again.

His wife had known about Billy for six hours before Thomas knew. Thomas could not imagine what those six hours had been for Nicole. Why didn't I have the car phone with me? he thought. Why didn't I call in?

He wanted to hold Nicole, and to be held, but she was asleep, having been given a tranquilizer from a doctor.

What doctor? thought Thomas.

The Williamses didn't have doctors. Nobody in their family ever got sick. Billy was never sick. How could Billy be dead when he had never even had the flu?

Thomas wanted to hold Laura, but holding her was strange and terrible. She was his only living child. She was all the children he had now. There was no Billy to hold. Billy, who would still, on special and rare occasions, allow his father to cuddle him.

Thomas could think of nothing to say to Laura. (*It's okay. Everything will be all right. We'll fix it.*)

No. It wasn't okay.

It would not be all right.

He could not fix it.

He tried to say things to his daughter (*Laura, are you okay, honey? I'm sorry I wasn't here. I love you, Laura*), but the only name he could manage was Billy's.

40

And the police said, "We need to ask some questions, Mr. Williams."

The questions were hard to hear, hard to decipher, as if they were really questions for somebody else, a test somebody else had studied for. "This morning," he said thickly, "I finished shutting down the factory at Darlington." Horrible. The city of Darlington desperately needed the jobs his company provided. But the company was losing too much money. Staying open was not possible.

"Did the workers get ugly?" asked the policeman.

Thomas didn't want to talk about it. Of course it had been ugly. Losing your income was an ugly thing.

"How would they know I had any family," he said wearily, "let alone decide to stalk my son and kill him? I cannot believe they would think of such a thing. Anyway, it's too quick. They couldn't even make the drive to London, let alone plan a bombing." His head throbbed hideously. Surely this could not be his fault. It could not be related to his work. Please, God, don't let my son be dead because of my actions.

He wanted Nicole to wake up.

Then he thought: what if she thinks this, too? What if my wife thinks our son is dead because I ended people's jobs?

"Tell us about the other places you shut down," said the police.

Thomas wanted to defend himself, and discuss the economy, and point out how his company had no choices, and how it wasn't his choice, anyway, merely his assignment.

But perhaps he had no defense. "Well, there was Northern Ireland," he said, and everybody looked up.

Northern Ireland. Where the harshest group of freedom fighters (their view) or murdering terrorists (the London view) was the IRA. A group not afraid to kill the unknown or the innocent. A group that dealt in bombs. A group whose expenses were often paid by Irish Americans—Boston Irish Americans. Both the escapees had been members of the IRA.

The Williamses were part Irish and came from Boston?

"Tell us," said the police, "about the Irish."

The phone rang constantly.

The police answered it.

Laura and Billy, who loved phone calls, would vault over furniture and throw stuff at each other to cut the other one's speed, trying to be first to answer.

There was no need to rush now.

Laura's friends called.

Con. Eddie. Tiffany. Mohammed. Bethany. Andrew.

Laura talked to Con, but it was too hard. She didn't talk to any of the others. What was there to say?

She thought about them, though. Their lives had gone on. Today, they had had class. Taken notes. Changed in the locker room for gym. How could that be? How could Billy be dead and other people's lives didn't stop, too?

Her father went to lie down with Mom. He didn't sleep; he just couldn't be without her any longer. And Laura sat alone among the strangers, wondering how it had felt to Billy. Had he known what he held in his hand? How long had he known? A split second, or an eternity? Had it hurt? How long had it hurt?

Laura was wrong about school.

It was completely different that day.

By midmorning, most of the student body had been taken home.

Fathers and mothers rushed to L.I.A. from work, frantic with nerves, trying to decide how to react.

Terrorism did not seem to be the sort of thing to which you could *over*react.

There was not one parent at L.I.A. for whom the risk was worth it. A dead kid? Never. Not mine, they thought.

For the Americans, if this was the beginning of violent anti-Americanism, then it was time to roll. Billy's death was a lesson the parents would learn. Even if they loved London, and thought it was the best posting they'd ever had, they were considering arrangements to send kids to family in Missouri or Vermont.

Anti-Americanism.

Most people didn't believe that could be the reason.

The English were irked by having so many Americans and so much American stuff cluttering up their country, but would they put a bomb in a little boy's hand because they didn't like having McDonald's on the corner? Because they preferred old-fashioned British fish-and-chips there instead? No.

Of course, London was packed with people who were not English; angry separated people whose countries really did hate America. Whose countries considered America to be Satan. Would *they* put a bomb in a little boy's hand?

Somebody had.

As for the L.I.A. parents who weren't American, their fear went far deeper, and had far more history.

L.I.A. was a school filled with possible targets.

Kids whose fathers had supported the wrong dictator or the wrong general.

Kids whose fathers had left town with other people's millions.

Kids whose parents had not moved their money in diamonds or in oil, but in heroin.

Kids whose fathers sold arms and weapons and information, and had enemies everywhere, and in everything.

But why Billy Williams?

He was nobody.

The whole Williams family was nobody.

They were the dullest of Americans.

They had no money.

They had no power.
So what did it mean?
Who had done it?
Would they try it again?
And what child would they choose the second time?

CHAPTER

5

Once more, the man in the too-large suit told Laura his name. "Mr. Evans," she repeated, trying to hold it. "I need facts."

"Miss Williams, we don't have facts yet. It's a guessing game now. We will start by investigating terrorists whose style is that sort of bomb."

"Style?" she said. "Terrorists have style?"

He began to discuss techniques of terrorism, but Laura couldn't bear it. She didn't want Billy to be part of a string of deaths; a mere entry in a series. She wanted a *reason*.

"I want you to leave now, Mr. Evans," she said in a high, thready voice she did not recognize as her own. "You're done here," she said shrilly. She tried to shoo the police out of the flat.

Their flat was on the second floor of a brick row house that looked like a Mary Poppins picture. The front of the block bowed and curved romantically. The roofs were orange tile and onion domes decorated the corners. Each house had its own tiny front garden, and when they said "garden" here, they meant it: roses were in bloom right now, in mid-November.

The flat had a living room and a dining room and a funny little kitchen with the smallest appliances in history—a refrigerator that a kid in a college dorm would laugh at, and a washing machine that barely held a pair of jeans. The three bedrooms had no closets.

You kept your clothes in a wardrobe.

Laura had wondered what a wardrobe was ever since she had read *The Lion, the Witch and the Wardrobe*. It turned out to be a freestanding wooden closet, a huge piece of furniture. Laura didn't know how they'd gotten the wardrobes into the flat. Billy thought they must have used a derrick to bring them up through the windows. How Billy had grieved that he was too big to play hide-and-seek in the wardrobes. But then—oh joy!—Billy figured out how to dismantle them. Laura often came home to find her closet distributed throughout the flat.

The wonderful London flat was ruined now.

The flat had no Billy, but his traces remained, because Billy could not be in a room without leaving himself everywhere. The flat had the taste and feel of strangers with terrible messages. It had the media gathered on the street below, ruining Heathfold Gardens as well.

The rain came down harder. The temperature

dropped, and the rain turned to sleet. When she went to bed, Laura listened to it beating on the roof tiles. She thought of Billy's room.

Empty.

She thought of Billy's bed.

Empty.

Laura's eyes would not close. Her body felt as if sleep had departed permanently. She wasn't going to do sleep again, any more than she would do first grade again.

The days went by.

The Williams family did not give interviews. They would not get in camera range. They did not discuss their grief. They did not offer up home movies or photographs of their dead little boy.

The funeral service was private, and the media never found out where or when it had taken place.

In a few days, the media gave up on Heathfold Gardens.

The Consul General of the U.S. Embassy handled the deaths of Americans abroad, including the undertaker, the coroner, and shipment of the body. In Billy's case, it was pieces of body.

Laura knew that death was death, and so it didn't matter how badly the body was torn, but it *did* matter. That Billy was not whole in death mattered terribly. She wanted a surgeon to put him back together.

She was even living in the land of nursery rhymes. The land of Humpty Dumpty. Indeed, all the king's horses and all the king's men could not put Billy together again. Laura even had all the king's men: Scotland Yard filled her flat and stood on her street and questioned Billy's classmates.

And they put nothing back together.

And never would.

Terrorism, whether there is one victim or a hundred, earns its name. People are terrified.

London quaked.

People were frightened on the tube, nervous on buses, edgy at traffic circles, tense in crowds, uncertain on trains.

People just wanted it to go away, and not get close to them.

The victim was American. Maybe it was his own fault. If foreigners would just go home, maybe these things would not happen. London seemed more than usually full of foreigners: people you could not trust; people who would kill a stranger.

Eventually it was necessary to go to the grocery.

Laura and Nicole could not avoid the aisles that included Marmite and digestive biscuits, two disgusting foods that English people seemed genuinely fond of, and Billy had been determined to like also. (He failed.)

Laura got milk, packaged in a container Billy insisted was a bleach bottle, and he was always telling his mother that he'd like another glass of Clorox, please.

There at the meat counter was hamburger, which British butchers ground too large for Billy; he said it looked like earthworms, so Nicole had to have the beef reground.

Today the butcher smiled. He'd seen Mrs. Williams coming, and had her meat ready. The butcher had not connected the bombing across town with the little American kid who was always demanding special attention. Any minute now, the butcher would ask where Billy was. Laura's mother fled down the aisle before she had to hear the words, so Laura took the package and said, "Thank you," and he said, "Where's your brother?" and she couldn't manage, "He's dead," so she said, "Not here today."

Or any day.

She had to force her mother through the checkout.

They went home, and the mail had come, full of letters from home. Home meaning America.

Nicole and Laura had gotten few letters since they'd moved abroad. Everybody from home wanted to visit, but nobody wanted to write. "I don't write letters," they would say smugly, as if this made them better people. (I don't chew tobacco, I don't rip up the flag, I don't write letters.) *Now*, when Billy wasn't there to shout, "Mail! I get to open it!"—*now*, they wrote.

Laura's mother put the condolence letters in a basket on the coffee table without opening them. "I don't care how sorry people are," she said raggedly. "I'm angry with them. Their sons are alive."

Laura turned on the television for distraction and regretted it. Billy had liked English soap operas in which people swore at each other in Cockney. "Shuddup, guv, gimme ya bleedin' quid er I'll bleedin' well knock ya head in." But all three of them had become addicted to *Neighbors,* an Australian soap. Billy liked to mutter the actors' lines as the show progressed so he could acquire a good Australian accent. "It'll come in handy," he explained, "for when I'm a spy."

Neighbors was on.

Laura and her mother cried in front of the television.

The family was flat and one-dimensional without Billy. Soda with the cap left off. The fizz was gone.

The British police kept suggesting that they should return to America. Thomas's company wanted him home, too. They flew a couple of executives to London to coax. But neither parent was ready. They needed to be near Billy still. Being in London made them feel they were accomplishing something.

On Sunday, the Williams family went to church.

Church in England was so different from church at home. In a New England Congregational Church, the service was simple: three hymns and a sermon. In London, there were Episcopal services, where the choir wore astonishing robes with fur trim, and the priest intoned canticles, and the people stood and sat and knelt and rose all through the service, and you needed an entire separate book just to follow what you did during that hour.

The only part Laura was sure of was the Lord's Prayer.

She said it by heart. How familiar were the gentle words. How welcome. Her mouth said a line she had always liked: *"Forgive us our trespasses, as we forgive those who trespass against us."*

Laura had been brought up on this. Be nice. Forgive. Forget. Put aside the ugly things other people do to you, and in exchange, they will forget the ugly things you do to them.

Congregation, choir, and priests said it together, in soft private voices that turned into one public voice: *"Forgive us our trespasses, as we forgive those who trespass against us."*

And suddenly Laura could not stand it. What a stupid wrong wrong sentence! Why were sensible people repeating that stupid sentence—week in and week out!—pretending it was correct? Pretending it was valuable? And worthy?

"Forgive us our trespasses, as we forgive those who trespass against us."

Her parents stumbled on through the prayer. They were stumbling through their lives now, too, unable to pick up their feet or their hearts or their words. It seemed to Laura that her parents were living in rented bodies, whose parts didn't work well, and whose speech was erratic.

Laura's mother was spending hours each day on the phone with Grandma, desperate for the comfort of her own mother's voice, but what could comfort her? No matter how dear Grandma's voice, Billy remained where he was. Gone.

Nicole was crying again. Little drops of rain fell on the prayer book. Thomas did not see. He was blind inside his own grief.

Forgive Billy's killer?

Laura Williams shuddered as if Billy's heart and soul had moved through her.

And Laura Williams said out loud, *"Never."*

CHAPTER 6

One week after the murder, Thomas went back to work.

Mr. Evans took Laura to school. Laura did not ask why. She had become fond of Mr. Evans, glad when he dropped in every day. Going to school with him seemed quite natural.

It was ugly out. Raw and rainy. Ordinary London weather.

Laura wore a long crimson wool skirt, black boots, and a high-necked black sweater. Over this, she wore her flannel-lined denim jacket. Laura rarely used a purse, but stuffed bus pass, snack money, and pencils into her jacket pockets.

Denim was so American.

Even though American blue jeans were very popular abroad, Laura could always tell who was American and who was foreign but wearing American jeans. Sometimes she mixed up Australians or Canadians, until they talked, and she got the accent, but she never mixed up English or Europeans. They just didn't wear denim the same way.

Laura had considered wearing the no-color raincoat that was a London specialty. Indeed, Americans came to London just to purchase such a raincoat. Raincoats blended into the crowds.

When you lived abroad, you found out that some stereotypes were true. Americans did talk louder, laugh harder, and swing their bodies more than the British. British posture was condensed. American posture, in comparison, was a swagger. Americans took up more space on the sidewalk than the English did.

Laura was surprised at her own fashion statement, wearing that denim jacket, unwilling to blend. Surprised that she was going out of her way to walk American, as if she owned the sidewalk. *Yes. I'm an American. Wanna make something of it? Wanna kill me, too?*

Laura made conversation—loud, like American tourists, using the vowel-switch Boston accent she did not really possess.

Mr. Evans went with her into the high school building. Billy had not had classes there. Middle school rooms were separated by the cafeteria, and sixth graders had lunch at a different hour. But Billy had been too boisterous to go unnoticed, and everybody in high school had known him, anyway. You couldn't help knowing him. His presence was noisy and full of energy, and people smiled when they heard him, even when he was being his most annoying.

Laura and Mr. Evans were met by the headmaster, Mr. Frankel. Mr. Frankel was beyond flustered. He was scared.

One of his students had been slain. Within hours, dozens of his students had bailed out, quitting to attend another school or leaving the country entirely. Was Mr. Frankel going to be stranded here with a building and no students? Of course it had to be *other* families with enough sense to go home. The Williams family, the dangerous ones, were staying.

"Laura, are you sure you're ready?" said Mr. Frankel, who was not ready. Mr. Frankel had moved to London the same year that thirty people had been incinerated in King's Cross Underground Station. Terrorism. The thought of terrorism in his very own school turned him into a Ping-Ping ball, bouncing on the table of his fears. He was responsible for so many children.

Yes, the school had bomb drills, but nobody expected to *find* bombs! Yes, the school had locks, television monitors, and armed patrols, but nobody expected to *need* this stuff. And what blockade would that be to a terrorist, anyhow? Obviously, none.

"Your brother's death, I'm sure," said Mr. Frankel, hoping even now that Laura Williams would just go home, "is very, very difficult to face, and—"

"I'm ready," said Laura.

o   o   o

Nicole Williams watched her daughter dress, and then watched from the window as Mr. Evans and Laura went up Heathfold Gardens toward the bus stop on Finchley Road.

Nicole had always been able to believe that she was Billy's mother. Billy coming home from school was an event. He never walked in: he sprang or raced or vaulted. He never had time to sit down for milk and cookies, but had to snack standing up because he had so much to tell, so many bartered treasures to show off, and a desperate need for cash, to buy something that couldn't wait another half hour.

Nicole had never quite believed, however, that she was Laura's mother. Back when Laura was short and scrawny with braces on her teeth and hair falling out of a ponytail, yes. But this tall, slender young woman with the romantic eyes and the sense of fashion from Paris? Nicole could never believe it was school Laura had been attending. Laura must have been at Cinderella's ball.

Nicole finished her coffee. She stared into the open kitchen cabinet where the coffee can belonged. Next to it sat cans of SpaghettiOs. Nicole made a superior tomato sauce; it took four hours and would make an Italian weep. Billy preferred SpaghettiOs.

In England, they stuck their spaghetti on toast, cut it into chunks, and ate it upside down off the backs of their forks. It was enough to make you throw up.

Billy thought it was awesome. Billy wanted to eat just like the English, and sometimes entire dinners were spent yelling at Billy to hold his fork right side up.

"But why?" Billy would ask. "Do you think you're being rational?" ("Rational" was on his sixth-grade vocabulary list. Billy took his vocabulary lists seriously.)

"Billy," Thomas would say, "if you argue with your mother once more, you're in deep—"

Nicole would frown.

"Trouble," Thomas would finish reluctantly.

"Daddy," Billy would say happily, "you almost used a swear. That would be contravening Mom's bye laws."

In the kitchen, alone with her empty coffee mug, Nicole wept into her hands. Billy, you contravened my bye laws. You were supposed to stay alive.

She picked up a can of SpaghettiOs and threw it across the room. "This is what I have left of you, Billy!" she shouted. "Why did you take that package? Why didn't you throw it into the crowd? I don't care about that woman or that baby! I care about *you!*"

She folded down on the counter, sobbing.

She tried to tell herself that it was a good thing Billy had used his own body to shelter the innocent, but Nicole had given birth to Billy's body, and the end of that body was *not* a good thing.

Oh! How she wished she could have gone with him. Wherever Billy was now, eleven was too young to be there.

o   o   o

Blessed school.

It swung you along in its particular rhythm, and you had no choices. You sat at your desk in one class, and then you got up and walked to your desk in the next. Teachers talked and blackboards were written upon and papers were passed out and bells rang.

Laura did not focus on anything that was said, but time passed, and that alone was a blessing.

Everybody talked to her—everybody who had not fled because of the bombing. Julie was gone. Kathleen Marie was gone. Michael the Ten was gone, leaving Kyrene, who had adored him.

The remaining students were awkward around Laura. Americans could hug, but they could think of no words. Middle Easterners were more graceful in their speech and often spoke decoratively, with long, ornate sentences. But kids from anywhere had trouble figuring out what to say to the sister of dead Billy Williams.

Laura loved them for struggling.

At lunch, however, everybody stuck like traffic on Billy's death. And like a traffic jam, they just wished the mess of his death would go away. Now Laura hated them.

She hated the good manners on which she had been brought up (and which had escaped Billy). Her mother would have commanded Laura to comfort her friends and assure them that she was okay.

Laura was having tuna fish on American white bread, the kind Billy approved of. She was afraid to pick up the sandwich. She would crush it. Tuna and mayo would spurt between her fingers.

Kyrene brought up the Thanksgiving dance. She said how awful it was that Michael had left L.I.A. and could not take her; how heartbroken she was.

Laura had to concentrate on opening her paper napkin and smoothing the folds, or she would have screamed at Kyrene: *You fool! Michael's nothing but a date! It doesn't matter! He's not dead!*

Eddie had the nerve to fondle her hair, in the old way, as if life were still ordinary. "Laura, I want you to come to the dance with me," he said.

"Eddie, I'm going to have you arrested if you touch my hair once more."

"Oh," said Eddie sorrowfully. "Does this mean you aren't coming with me?" In spite of the warning, he tried to touch her hair again.

That settled it. Laura was wearing her hair up from now on. It would give her mother something to do in the morning. Braids and twists.

Lunch chatter went on, and Laura found herself sliding into it after all. Perhaps normalcy lurked everywhere. The moment you relaxed your defenses, up it stood, trying to make you forget your mission: finding Billy's killer.

"Thanksgiving confuses me," said Mohammed.

"The turkey and the Pilgrim and the cranberry. Where does it lead, and why are we dancing?"

Mohammed was a Ten and a Half. Possibly even an Eleven. Nobody could better fit the horoscope ideal of a tall, dark, handsome stranger. Laura had often imagined herself dancing the night away with Mohammed.

Now she could see that Mohammed was excellent in all ways, but she could no longer see why this might matter.

She wanted very much to speak to God. *How did you decide that a Mohammed or a Kyrene gets to go on living, but not Billy?* she would demand of God.

The answer came as clearly as if He had spoken. *A terrorist made that decision, Laura, not me.*

She thought of the terrorism that had happened in Oklahoma City, and the bombing of the Federal Building, where vicious, selfish, evil doers had murdered tiny children and ordinary office workers. She looked at her ordinary classmates. She could not see them clearly.

What Laura saw, instead, were those who had left L.I.A. Guilty people fled. Were the absent kids, therefore, guilty? Did they know something? Or not want to know something? Or were they just prudent—going while they could?

Is who *left* important? she thought. Or is who *stayed* important?

The collection of kids at this table was most unusual: Con, Andrew, Tiffany, Jehran, Eddie, Kyrene, Mohammed, Jimmy, and Bethany. Jimmy had a different set of friends; Jehran wasn't fond of Americans; Tiffany was too snobbish; Kyrene had always been with Michael.

"You don't usually dance for Thanksgiving, Mohammed," said Con.

What a lot of thinking Laura had accomplished between Mohammed's question and Con's answer. She must be getting her thinking capacity back. That was good; she had a terrorist to find—but where to start? There were no clues here, just people whose routines had been interrupted, whose friendships had ended, and for whom crowding together for lunch felt better than sitting alone.

"I've never heard of a Thanksgiving dance, actually," Con continued. "It's because we aren't home, and turkeys are hard to find in London groceries, and not everybody can go over the river and through the woods to Grandma's house, so on Friday they're having a dance to make up for it."

The Americans grinned because they knew what Con was saying. Nobody else understood a word. Foreigners would never sort Thanksgiving out. It was an All-American secret.

The old sweet tune sang in Laura's head: *"Over the river and through the woods to Grandmother's house we go . . ."*

Grandma was begging them to come home for

Thanksgiving. She herself wasn't well enough to fly to England. Grandma had to use a walker now because her knees buckled. Every morning she gulped down trays of medication to keep her ailing heart and lungs and joints working. And now her only grandson was dead, and Laura's parents refused to leave London.

"Because," Thomas would say hopelessly. "Because . . . Billy's still here, somehow."

Jehran was listening intently to the Thanksgiving discussion.

Jehran had fascinated Billy. Not her perfume, hair, clothing, speech—all of which were exotic and beautiful—but the fact that she arrived at school in a bullet-proof limousine. Billy loved that. One of his lists had been Students Who Come to School in Limousines. To Jehran's limousine, Billy added *bullet-proof.*

The police had Billy's lists. Laura was suddenly afraid Mr. Evans would lose the lists; this important part of Billy would drop behind some gray desk and vanish. Her breath caught in her chest, and she had difficulty swallowing and needed to find a telephone and tell Mr. Evans to drive over here with the lists.

Handsome, blond, American Andrew (a definite Ten) leaned across the table and steered among abandoned sandwich crusts to touch Laura's hand. People were being social workers around the Williamses. The advice from American friends to her mother was: do normal things. Bit by bit you'll find yourself back in a routine.

Why would anybody want a routine without Billy?

Actually, now that Laura thought about it, Billy had had many routines; he was a person who loved repetition.

"Laura," said Andrew, giving her a sweet, grave smile, "if you're ready to get out of the house a little, I'd love to take you to the Thanksgiving dance."

Laura could not get over that her friends did not see the gaping, shrieking hole of rage that Billy's death had ripped in her heart. Everybody at this table (except Jehran, whose Moslem family would never condone such an Americanism as dating) was still thinking of boy-girl activities, while she, Laura, was thinking of revenge.

"Why would she want to do that, Andrew?" said Tiffany crossly. "It's way too early. Billy's hardly in his grave."

Laura did not like Tiff, but there was some annoying requirement when you were out of your country that you had to be nice to your fellow Americans. Even if, like Tiffany, they were worthless fellow Americans.

On the other hand, you could be worthless and still be right.

"She's gonna dance around the room when her brother's just been splatted on a moving stair?" demanded Tiff.

"I'm sorry," said Andrew, horrified. "I didn't mean Laura should celebrate. I meant going to the dance could be a rest."

A dreadful thought stood up in front of Laura's eyes. She did not see Andrew turn for forgiveness and she did not see Tiffany turn for confirmation.

What if Billy's killer was somebody in school? Somebody right here at L.I.A.?

After all, school had been the majority of Billy's life. He'd been headed to school when he died. His lists were mostly school lists, and his friends had been entirely school friends.

What did she really know about these kids?

This international set had lived all over the world, not just Hong Kong and Paris and Helsinki, but also stints in Houston and Cincinnati and Atlanta. Plenty of kids from different nations were as good at being American as Laura. Andrew, who seemed so American: Did she know for sure? Andrew could be lying. With that white-blond hair, he could be from Scandinavia, not an American descended from somebody from there.

But did you have terrorists from Norway?

Weren't terrorists sort of country-specific?

Where was Mr. Evans when she needed him? She had a thousand new questions to ask.

"Where is Billy buried, anyway, Laura?" asked Tiffany, who was on a roll. "You ship the body back to Massachusetts? You didn't bury him here in England, did you? I mean, won't you want to be able to visit the grave after you get home?"

Everybody was shocked, even people who expected the worst from Tiffany.

Con, the diplomat's child, rushed to share a bag of Cape Cod Potato Chips, flown in by her aunt. Airmail potato chips worked out to about fifteen dollars a bag. People crunched gratefully, covering Tiffany's rudeness and Laura's silence.

Why was Tiffany full of questions? What if everything Tiffany had said about her family was a lie? And Eddie? And Andrew? And Mohammed? Even her best friend, Con? Who were they, really?

Laura's eyes burned, dimly seeing the outline of killers where before she had had friends.

CHAPTER 7

At last Laura Williams had an Extracurricular Activity. Day after day she pursued her new interest.

Bet "Finding My Brother's Killer" doesn't show up that often on college admission essays, thought Laura, knowing the essay would be worth writing only if she found him.

School gave Laura a fever. She was hot and shivery from staring at her former friends. She tried to turn them inside out; inspect their secrets and their pasts. There was no time to eat lunch, only time to sit in the cafeteria and examine faces.

Jimmy Hopkins, for example, seemed worth pursuing. He looked Japanese, but his name certainly didn't fit.

The eyes of a terrorist should be cold and amoral, unblinking and uncaring. Eyes to be afraid of. But in the eyes of Jimmy Hopkins, she could see only curiosity and pity.

"Jimmy," she said sharply, "where are you from?"

"Los Angeles," said Jimmy courteously. He ate his chips like a Londoner: squishing the head of each french fry into a puddle of vinegar and salt.

"But what are you, really?" said Laura. "What nationality?"

"I'm American," he said, trying to be patient. Laura had interrogated almost everybody; he had known his turn was coming. "You want the whole nine yards? A Hawaiian grandmother who was part Japanese and part New England missionary married an Irish grandfather. That's my mother's side. I have an Italian grandmother and an origin-unknown grandfather on my father's side."

"That's not enough Japanese blood to look as Japanese as you do."

"So speak to my gene pool," said Jimmy irritably. He took the remains of his sandwich to the trash can and got in line for dessert.

"Stop testing people, Laura," murmured Con, tilting back in her metal chair until she was so close to Laura that conversation was muffled in each other's hair. Con, as always, looked perfect. She was not beautiful or even pretty, yet she was a Ten in any numbering system. "Billy wasn't killed by anybody at school, Laura. I know you're upset, but don't be melodramatic."

"Murder," said Laura, "*is* melodramatic. When you're murdered by being handed your own personal bomb, it is *very* melodramatic. Billy was somebody's choice, Con! He was handed his own murder weapon! He had to carry his own death up a stair."

Every time Laura imagined it, she wanted to yank Billy to safety; her muscles seemed to believe there was still time to do this.

Con nodded understandingly—as if a person who used the word "upset" for Billy's death could understand. "I'm sorry, Laura," said Con. "You're right. It is melodrama. It could be on stage, or be a movie."

"No! You don't get it! It isn't a screenplay. It's my brother!"

The whispered conversation exhausted Laura. Her strength was dwindling away, just when she needed it most. She had lost rest completely. Her sleep had become a strange shallow thing, a mere trembling on top of sheets.

"It makes me angry you even thought of anybody in school," scolded Con. "I love this school. It's terrible of you to think that way."

The only way outsiders could tolerate the way Billy died was to make it ordinary. People who could not make Billy's death ordinary had left.

Laura knew that she was ending friendships left and right. Her life used to be based on making, keeping, and strengthening friendships. No longer. She had abandoned sleeping, eating, and friendliness.

"Practically speaking," added Con, "who could pull it off, Laura? They don't teach a class in bombs."

"Well, then, the bomb was made by their father, or their uncle, or their president, or their dictator." Mentally Laura examined a geography class globe. Peeling away the three quarters that were ocean, she sorted through land. How many countries was she talking about? How many fathers, uncles, presidents, and dictators?

It was too big a task. Laura could never do it. They had beaten her before she began.

For a moment, she had no energy with which to go on. Then she remembered the only time you don't have the energy to go on is when you're dead. So only Billy did not have the energy to go on. She, Laura, must go on for him.

Jimmy came back with not one, but two desserts, and the second one he put in front of Laura. It was cake, European style, with many thin layers and thin, crusty icing. Billy's idea of cake was chocolate, with soft icing an inch thick. Laura did not say thank you for the cake. She asked Jimmy for proof that he was American. His driver's license, or his passport.

"You know, Laura," said Jimmy, yanking the cake back, "somebody is going to mug you. Now quit this crap."

"I have to find out who killed Billy."

"You think somebody's going to tell you?" yelled Jimmy. Half the cafeteria turned. " 'Oh, rats, Laura, you got me, I'm from a terrorist family.' "

Laura flushed. She didn't know how to be a spy and

find out things. She was as blunt and imperfect as Billy. Jimmy was right. Who would tell her anything? Nobody.

Laura pretended to have finished lunch, pretended to saunter off, but she was running away, and when she got into the hall, she did run. Nobody was after her; she was running away from being a jerk. She stood hidden in a corner of contradictory doorways that led in and out of the music rooms.

Laura was not musical and did not participate in choir or band, but the music rooms were centrally located, so against their will, she and everybody else knew what the Christmas concert was going to include. They had known since September.

Leila and Avram were practicing a duet. Leila was Syrian and played the violin, while Avram was Israeli and played the cello.

Weren't Syria and Israel mad at each other? Didn't they have different religions and different politics and argue about their borders and hate each other? What were Leila and Avram doing playing a Christmas carol together? Laura thought of Syria as primitive and Israel as sophisticated, and both had terrorists.

What nationalities were in Billy's grade? Had he gotten mixed up in some Israeli-Syrian mess? Some Irish-English mess?

In the months she had lived abroad, Laura had not made the slightest effort to understand what those messes were, or which side stood for what.

I'm ignorant, thought Laura. I was proud of being

ignorant. I felt superior because I *didn't* know anything. When you're an American, and you're the best and the strongest, you don't have to worry what all those little guys are up to.

Laura had tired quickly of British television news. The BBC told you about every single political party in every single country on every single continent. Just when you thought you were going to go into a coma, you would find out about the royals. A princess was bound to have visited an old folks home, or else Australia, or else was getting a divorce. Then it was back to global news.

Time to be like the English and learn political situations, thought Laura.

So instead of being late for current events, Laura was early.

Naturally Mr. Hollober loved it that a student had come to hear his wisdom. He straddled the high wooden stool on which he liked to perch. "Civilization can vanish pretty fast," he began. "Look at Yugoslavia. Sarajevo was a lovely town. The Winter Olympics were held there, but a minute later—as time goes— neighbors were killing each other off as fast as they could reload the rifles. Bosnia is a nightmare of terrorism against one's own."

Laura did not want to get into the Philosophy of Neighborliness. She wanted to cut to the chase. "Which country has terrorists?" she said abruptly.

Mr. Hollober shrugged. "Terrorists are just criminals. Evil people who kill for selfish reasons. Every country has its criminals." Mr. Hollober folded himself up: fingers, knees, and elbows tucked in tight. His students joked that he could lecture only in fetal position. "The difference is, terrorists think they're good guys. Terrorists believe they are changing the world, not just damaging it."

"I don't want details, Mr. Hollober. Just a list of who has terrorists." Laura was normally courteous to her teachers, partly because she had been raised to speak politely, and partly because she never wanted to jeopardize a grade. I'm beyond grades, she thought, the way I'm beyond friendship.

Mr. Hollober regarded her for some time without saying a word. What if he decided not to tell her? "I have to know," she explained, "because I believe somebody in this school had something to do with my brother's death."

"Don't be ridiculous!" Mr. Hollober was personally offended, as if anybody at London International Academy was an automatic Good Citizen. After all, they had studied current events with *him*.

"Think about it," Laura said. "What did Billy do all day long? He went to school. Right here. With these kids."

Mr. Hollober lost it. He jumped up from his neat folds and loomed over her. His voice was sharp and angry. "He also wandered all over London, Laura! Your parents let him do *anything!* He stole bricks from construction sites! Took photographs! Kept notes! Asked questions! Bothered people! Went right up to strangers! He was one very invasive little boy!"

Laura could hardly breathe. She wanted to deck the man. *"Are you saying it was Billy's own fault he got murdered?"*

"No, Laura. I'm saying he could have stumbled onto anything, anywhere. Billy Williams was completely unsupervised."

Now the man dared blame her mother and father. She would never attend current events again.

Laura turned on her heel and spun out of the classroom, ran down the ugly open stairs that belonged in a lighthouse, ran down the carpeted halls papered with art class garbage, ran toward the nearest exit, ran up to the door to shove her hand against the push bar—ran into Mohammed.

Mohammed caught the exit door before she got it open. "Laura, you of all people must not go outside without your bodyguard."

"My bodyguard?" She was completely astonished.

"Mr. Evans," said Mohammed.

Laura thought of Mr. Evans as a pleasant, middle-aged, fatherly policeman. Body. Guard. A person to guard your body. A person to make sure nobody blew you up.

How Billy would have loved it. His sister had a bodyguard.

"Oh Mohammed," she whispered. And she was not

angry, not vengeful. She was just tears and loss. "Billy could have every one of my Twinkies if I could just have him back."

Mohammed nodded. "My Twinkies, too."

She cried for a while and then she found a tissue in her pocket and mopped her face. Billy of course had never considered the use of a tissue. He loved his sleeve. He said runny noses reinforced the fabric. Little boys were so disgusting.

She smiled, thinking how much she would like the privilege of yelling at Billy for being disgusting.

"What are Twinkies?" said Mohammed then, smiling also.

Laura shook her head. There were times when you had the energy to explain American stuff and times when you didn't.

One day, Con had brought Laura a bag of American snacks that you could not buy in London but that Con, because her father worked at the embassy, could get from the commissary: Twinkies, Mallomars, and Peppermint Patties. Laura locked herself in the bathroom to keep Billy from stealing her precious snacks. Billy wrote messages on Kleenex and poked them under the bathroom door with a pencil tip. HAVE PITY ON ME, I AM STARVING.

Laura wrote back with lipstick on toilet paper. CANNOT FIT TWINKIES UNDER DOOR. Billy stuck his tongue under the door, imploring her to put Twinkie crumbs on it. "Mop my tongue with Twinkie filling," he moaned. Laura tried, but the filling scraped off when Billy pulled his tongue back.

Mohammed was so much taller than Laura that her eyes were level with his chest and she could not see past him. Mohammed was so solid. His seemed a body that nothing could destroy. But she would have said that of Billy, too: there was too much personality in Billy for a mere bomb to take him. "Oh, Mohammed," said Laura, "we can't have him back. I still can't believe it's true."

"Here is another thing that is true," said Mohammed. "Your parents need you, Laura. You must be careful for yourself. You must not rob them of their other child."

Laura hated being told how to behave. "I have things to do," said Laura, her hand going to the push-bar.

"Laura, stop it. Don't be such an American. This is not a game."

"Oh, you Arabs," said Laura, "you just want to push people around."

"Oh, we Arabs," said Mohammed, "would like our friends to behave rationally and not endanger themselves."

One of the differences between American kids and foreign kids was age. Kids like Mohammed always seemed older, as if they had suffered more, or understood it better. Americans expected more good things from life: more comfort, more fun. Other people expected less.

Billy had expected everything, always.

"I want to go into the tube station," said Laura, "and see where it happened."

In a voice as even and smooth as his olive complexion, Mohammed said, "I don't think that is a good idea."

His accent was American. Most kids at L.I.A. could talk American. Imitating American was in. You had to have American sneakers and American jeans, listen to American rock groups and eat American french fries. Above all, you had to use American slang exactly right.

But he was not American.

"What country are you from, Mohammed?" she asked.

"Palestine."

She was exasperated. "That's not a country."

Mohammed did not react like an American. He didn't make a face or swear or tell her where to go. He said gravely, "It is to me."

"It's Israel. It's been Israel since before my father was born."

Mohammed did not argue. He went back to the original question. "They've fixed the escalator at the tube stop, Laura. You can't tell that anything happened. If you want to go into the station, I will go with you. But you should not."

Israel, she thought, is like Northern Ireland. Just when you think the Israelis and the Palestinians are going to have peace, somebody throws a bomb. Is Mohammed a Palestinian who would throw a bomb?

She shook off such an awful idea. Mohammed was in her Shakespeare class. They had memorized lines together. It was impossible to imagine Mohammed planning the deaths of children. He was a wonderful person. She was ashamed, but the thought would not go away. "Is your passport Israeli, Mohammed?"

Back in Massachusetts, nobody even knew what a passport was. Vaguely you knew if you went to France or something, you needed one. But most people weren't even going to Boston, never mind France. A passport wasn't like a driver's license, that you cared about.

Here in London, however, the word "passport" had a certain strength. You could not leave a country without showing your passport at the airport or the harbor; nor could you enter the next country. You could not stay at a hotel without your passport. You could not cash a traveler's check.

Some passports were better than others. U.S. passports were best.

Mohammed seemed so remote that when he finally answered, it felt to Laura as if he really were in another country. "I don't have a passport," he said softly.

Laura didn't get it. You had to have a passport.

Mohammed shook his head. "Quite a few kids at L.I.A. don't have papers. We're not here legally."

Laura was stunned. She had not known there was such a thing as wealthy illegals. Illegals were poor peasants who crept over borders in the dark and went to live in slums. Mohammed was very wealthy. You could be rich and still be illegal? "Does the school know?" she whispered.

"They look the other way."

"What would happen if you got caught?"

"Rich illegals don't get caught."

What a motto, thought Laura.

"It's the reason I'm not going on the class trip to France in January with the rest of you," said Mohammed. "I can't get into France, and if I did, I couldn't get back into England."

Some kids didn't go to Europe because they couldn't? They had all the money in the world—and were prisoners? Laura could hardly process this information. "But Mohammed, how did you get here to start with? Do you have a fake passport?"

"Laura, stop asking questions. I like you. I understand Americans. I know they can't shut up. But you will cause trouble, asking the wrong questions of the wrong people." He touched her, unusual for a Moslem boy, resting a hand on her shoulder. It was not affection; it was guidance. "Laura, this is a school with secrets. You must let people keep their secrets." His eyes moved away and fastened onto some distant place of sorrow.

Laura's place of sorrow was not yet distant. Billy, as Tiffany had put it, was hardly in his grave. Laura began to weep again. "I'm sorry, Mohammed."

He could not know that she was apologizing for

thinking he was a terrorist. He thought it was because she had started to cry again. "A brother deserves tears, Laura. He deserves more than tears. But taking the stairs he died on . . . I still don't think it's a good idea."

"Then what *is* a good idea?" she said. "Mohammed, I have to find him!"

Mohammed thought "him" meant Billy. "Laura, if I may ask you, doesn't Christianity tell you where Billy is?"

Laura did not think of herself as a Christian, but as a Congregationalist, although she knew one was part of the other. She had been yelling at God for allowing this, but she had not asked Him who the terrorist was.

She didn't want to either. She wanted her God in a realm where only the keeping and cherishing of Billy counted.

The headmaster came pounding down the hall. Laura remembered now that Mr. Frankel could watch every corner of the school on his television monitors. He must have seen her cowering between doors near the music rooms.

"I want you both in class right now!" Mr. Frankel all but spat the syllables. His voice was way too angry.

Laura knew the feeling.

The problem was that the police, Scotland Yard, and the antiterrorist squad had discovered nothing. They did not know one more thing about Billy's death than they had known the first hour. Nobody claimed responsibility. Nobody who'd seen anything came forward. None of Billy's activities or collections led investigators anywhere. Explosives experts were examining fragments of Billy's bomb, but results were inconclusive.

Nothing is more frightening than nothing.

Even the slimmest clue would have comforted the headmaster, her parents, and Laura. But there was nothing.

She imagined the truth as nothing.

Billy as nothing.

God as nothing.

It was too terrible. There had to be something.

The terrorists of the world swirled in Laura's mind. Men full of rage. Men with weapons. Men with a Cause. Men who did not care about children.

I will suspect everybody. I will find my terrorist. Even if he is in my class. *Especially if he is in my class.*

CHAPTER 8

"**I**," said Jehran, the week after Thanksgiving, "am having a slumber party. Everybody must come."

The American girls were amazed. Slumber parties were so American—and so babyish. You were ten when you had slumber parties. But they were also thrilled. Jehran's life was a mystery. Jehran never invited Americans over, just Samira or one of the other Middle Eastern girls. Jehran was supposed to be one of the wealthiest students at L.I.A. Everybody said her gold and diamonds were gold and diamonds.

"I shall need instruction," said Jehran, "to grasp the rules of slumber parties." Jehran's speech was very British: the lovely, classy, television theater accent that Americans adored. Real-life Londoners rarely sounded that way. The Americans listened happily to Jehran's pretty sounds.

Con laughed. "Rule one—you don't sleep. Rule

two—you giggle all night long. Rule three—after midnight, you tell scary stories."

"No, no," said Kyrene, "the important thing is food. You cannot have a slumber party on a diet."

"That's for sure," said Tiffany. "I can eat Middle Eastern food if I have to, Jehran, but not all night long. Tell you what, I'll bring the real food."

Jehran lowered her lashes and looked through them, a reprimand everybody except Tiff found painful. When you were abroad, and an American was rude, you were responsible. Con said quickly, "We'll love whatever you serve, Jehran."

"Or pretend to," agreed Jehran, smiling.

It was a Euro-smile. Not broad and easy like American smiles, but thin with superiority. Euro-smiles made Laura crazy. She always wanted to say: *Listen, if you were really so good, you'd be number one in the world. And you're not. So there.*

She missed America.

The Williamses had had Thanksgiving dinner at the home of American friends, but there was nothing for which to be thankful. The day was fake, with the bag of Pepperidge Farm stuffing and the can for pumpkin pie flown in.

And who, Laura asked herself, who at L.I.A. is also fake?

Laura yearned to spot some tall, dark, evil stranger on whom to blame Billy's death. But she did not run into anybody she didn't already know. Nobody seemed to be eyeing her from cars or following her on sidewalks.

"Laura, you must come to my party," said Jehran, resting her hand on Laura's. "You need to laugh and smile."

Laura shook her head. "My parents need me."

This was a statement with which no Moslem would ever argue; parents were first. So when Jehran argued, the girls were amazed all over again. "Now, Laura," said Jehran. "At least ask your parents if you might come. We will be chaperoned. They need have no fear for your safety."

Samira sniffed. "American parents don't know what supervision is," she said. "They won't even think of asking whether there will chaperones, Jehran."

Jehran gave Samira a dirty look, remarkably like Billy when he didn't get his way, and turned her back on Samira. "You have sunk so low in your heart, Laura. We are your friends, and will spend our hours not in the telling of scary stories, but in the lifting of your heart."

Laura was touched by this little speech. Jehran was not particularly friendly, and yet she was the first to reach out and say, Come. Laura wanted to be polite, but she could not imagine going to a slumber party to giggle the night away. She shook her head.

"Can I help you, Mrs. Williams?" said Jimmy Hopkins.

The woman stood on the outside of the high, chain-link fence that enclosed the school playground. She had wrapped her fingers around the metal like a little kid who doesn't get to play, and was staring through the openings as if she thought Billy might be ready to come home.

He felt tender toward her, and very sad. "I'm Jimmy Hopkins," he reminded her. He didn't want to circle the fence to reach her; it would take him a few minutes, and she was too lost. He must stay by her side with the fence between them.

The television monitors that continually scanned the grounds had a use. The headmaster came swiftly out of the building and walked down the outside of the fence. "Hello, Mrs. Williams," said Mr. Frankel. "Laura is fine. Shall we go into my office and I'll call Laura down from class?"

It was not Laura Mrs. Williams was looking for. But she let Mr. Frankel lead her away. Her fingers bumped hopelessly along the chain links.

Jimmy forgave Laura everything.

"Can you believe it?" said Kyrene. "My parents might be transferred back to America. Washington, D.C. Isn't that pathetic? There's nothing to do in America but watch television."

Laura could not stand this kind of American. London was crammed with them: American kids who had never lived in America. They'd grown up in foreign countries and knew America from TV shows or by visiting relatives in the summer. They looked American. They talked American. But in some creepy way, they were not American.

"Expatriate" was the term. Sort of like ex-husband or ex-wife. They were ex-country. They had no use for America, (although they would never have surrendered their very useful American passports), and Laura despised them.

But she did not rouse herself to tell Kyrene off. Laura's speech was dwindling away. Nobody wanted to hear her talk about the only important thing: Billy's killer.

Jimmy, proving he was a Ten whether he looked like one or not, said to Kyrene, "Have I mentioned that if one more person says there's nothing to do in America but watch television, I'm going to shoot her?"

Several people laughed, but it wasn't funny. Loyalty wasn't funny, and no loyalty was less funny.

Who knew where the loyalties of expatriates lay? Laura thought. Expatriates would say terrible things about America, and the president, and the political party in control, and the way crime was so high, and people were amoral, and California was disgusting.

If they trashed their own country for nothing, what would such people do for pay?

For enough money, would they kill?

What if my first guess was wrong? thought Laura. What if it's not a foreigner who killed Billy? *What if it was an American?*

o   o   o

Thomas Williams pulled off the road.

He kept losing track of his destination, and having to sit for a moment and get his bearings. Oh yeah, he would think, staring at his map. Oh, yeah, I'm headed to Birmingham.

Then he would try to remember why anybody would want to go to Birmingham. He'd have to open his briefcase and leaf through his papers to jog his mind.

He was okay once he got wherever he was going. It was the journey that threw him. He could think only of his son's journey. Billy's last journey on earth, up a set of moving stairs . . . and then the final journey, where Thomas could not follow and could not help.

He could not stand it that no group claimed responsibility for Billy's death. He wanted somebody to blame this on. I could bury my son better, he thought, if there was a reason. A stupid reason, an evil reason—but at least a reason!

It cannot be chance. You don't hand out bombs by chance.

If he stayed close to where it had happened, Thomas thought, there was a possibility of figuring out the reason. But if the Williams family left, who would care anymore about Billy or the reason?

So Thomas was doomed to keep driving these English roads and ending these English jobs and living this English nightmare, even when everybody, including the company, wanted him home.

He still wanted to go to Russia for Christmas.

Laura, Tiff, and Andrew were the only students in French class who were not multilingual.

Laura could not imagine another language living inside her head and coming off her tongue. She wondered if speaking other languages made it easier to switch countries? Should she look for a person who could change tongues, and therefore loyalty and patriotism?

The teacher liked to work separately with each student because the class was on such different levels. The Americans, in foreign language, were at the bottom. Samira was summoned to the teacher's desk.

Jehran tried to entertain Laura by writing down the French conversions in Arabic. Arabic was a flowing vertical script, like the tide coming in, with flecks of spray dotted above. It was impossible to believe it had meaning.

Jehran was startlingly glamorous in comparison to the torn jeans and drab sweatshirts of American girls. She was very petite, almost childlike, yet wearing a brocade dress that Laura's mother would have found too mature. Jehran's thick hair hung down her back, black as a tuxedo.

"Jehran, *s'il vous plaît*," said the French teacher.

Jehran went up while Samira sat back down. Laura

remembered she hadn't asked about Samira's passport yet, so she did. "Laura, mind your manners," said Samira.

"I'm just asking if you're really American."

"I have never once claimed to be American," said Samira sharply, discarding her somewhat American accent and using the upper-class British accent Jehran had.

"It's the best passport," said Laura, figuring Samira would be forced to defend her real country now.

Sure enough, Samira snapped like a flag in the wind. "That's so American of you to think U.S. passports are better. Not everybody wants to live in New York or Los Angeles, you know. Some of us think you Americans are completely uncivilized. We want to stay here in Europe."

"But you're not European," said Laura, aiming for mild puzzlement. "What country are you from, Samira?"

Samira said with pride, almost with ferocity, "My grandfather was an advisor to the shah."

"The shah?" said Laura. The word meant nothing to her.

Laura was often the class dunce, so this surprised nobody. Andrew stepped in as tutor. "The shah was a king who once ruled Iran," he told Laura. "America supported the shah. He was overthrown way back in 1979, when the Shiite Moslems came to power. Shiites are very, very strict. The ruler they have now is called an ayatollah, a sort of Moslem priest. Iran hates America."

Laura was cross. She hadn't even been born when Samira's grandfather was advising this shah. How could such ancient history figure in Billy's death?

"The day will come," said Samira, "when my family will be restored to power. Then I can go home."

Home, thought Laura. I bet she wasn't even born there. She's my age; I bet the whole family left in 1979 and she's never even set foot in this place she calls home.

In America, when governments changed, people just lost their jobs. They gave a TV interview, left Washington, and went back to being lawyers in Texas.

But in Iran or Iraq—or Guatemala or Cambodia—the risk is higher. The next government may kill you. So the wealthy move to London.

I'm getting warm, thought Laura. People who murder are the ones I want.

But even as she traced the Arabic script Jehran had written, Laura reached another dead end. Terrorists would select *those* people to kill—Samira's grandfather, who supported the wrong guy. They wouldn't take Billy.

But they had.

Andrew felt responsible for Laura; attached to her in some deep, terrible way.

Only moments before the bomb went off, Andrew

had emerged safely from the Underground. He had felt the explosion through his feet and heard the sirens through his heart. Because of Chris and Georgie, who could identify clothes and book bag, it was quickly known that the victim was Billy Williams.

L.I.A. teachers and London transport police had ordered the students to go into the school building. American kids (not known for their obedience) had stayed where they were.

Andrew had stayed where Laura would get off the bus. Why? Had he hoped to be her knight in shining armor? He sure hadn't saved Billy, who had needed armor.

Or was terrorism exciting? And had Andrew wanted to be in on it?

It made Andrew's skin crawl to think that his mind could possibly be that crawly.

Andrew was struck by Laura's ignorance. How could Laura not know who the shah was? How could Laura not know what it meant that Samira's grandfather had supported the shah? Samira and her family could never go home. They had lost land and buildings and fortune, and very likely, lives. They had lost, period. They had no country.

Andrew's stomach heaved at the thought of having no country.

But Laura, making her little lists, understood nothing. She had no idea what terrible histories her classmates had. No idea that it was reasonable for such people to move about in bullet-proof cars.

Laura's unsophisticated, Andrew thought. And that's dangerous. She doesn't know enough. And that's dangerous.

Laura reminded Andrew of the continuous, metallic broadcasts at airports. *"Do not leave your luggage unattended."*

Laura was an unattended suitcase, waiting to be picked up. Picked up by who? A good-hearted neighbor like Andrew? Or a terrorist like . . .

Like who?

Laura stood with Eddie, waiting for the bus.

Billy had loved London buses and sat in the top front seat of double-deckers. Laura had heard an Englishman call that the tourist seat, so she refused to sit there because she wanted to look like a Londoner, not a tourist.

Billy liked to swing off the steps, or dance on the tiny stairs that led to the upper level, or corner a perfectly innocent rider and demand that the poor woman admire his latest card trick.

"Last time I took the 113 with Billy," said Laura, "the conductor said Billy needed a thump." The driver had been Jamaican, with a swingy musical voice.

"Did he thump Billy?" asked Eddie.

"No, but there were plenty of volunteers." Laura actually smiled, remembering Billy's agreeable laughter, how Billy introduced himself and yelled good-bye to the driver, whose name was Peter, and how Peter called, "Cheerio, Billy!" instead of thumping him, and Billy said, "See? I make friends with everybody. I never get thumped in the end."

Eddie picked up a newspaper from the many stacks at the kiosk next to the bus stop. Today, each London paper—the *Standard*, the *Telegram*, the *Times*—was head-lined "Terrorism."

Oh, no, please! What's happened now? With stiff fingers Laura handed coins to the vendor, who said "Cheers," same as "have a good day" in America. "Cheers," she said, wondering when she would ever have a good day again, and the headlines blurred when she tried to read the print.

"When I grow up, I'm going to do that," said Eddie.

"Do what?" Laura felt dizzy.

"Destroy Israel."

"What are you talking about?" said Laura.

He tapped the headlines with the back of his hand, like a drumroll. "Israel has no right to exist."

Laura managed to read some words. A bombing in Tel Aviv. Too far away for a Billy connection. "You're going to be a terrorist?" said Laura.

"No, I'm going to set Palestine free."

"You're Palestinian?"

"Certainly not," said Eddie, as if insulted. "But I hate Israel. Israel will end. I will assist."

A painful rasping quiver crept over Laura, as if Eddie's words had scraped the flesh off.

"Here's the bus," said Eddie with a smile. He gestured for her to precede him.

How nice, thought Laura, a terrorist who lets girls go first. But Eddie didn't hand Billy a bomb. Eddie was on the bus with me. So if Eddie's involved, somebody else actually threw it.

Could Eddie have waved to me that morning, and shared a seat, and talked about lunch, knowing that somebody was arranging for Billy to die?

Do I ride to school every morning with my brother's killer?

C H A P T E R

9

"**J**ehran is right," said Laura's father. "You do need to perk up, sweetie. I think you should go to the slumber party."

"Perk" sounded cute and freckled, as if Billy's death were a complexion problem. Laura tried not to be angry with her father. She was angry at so much now, she couldn't be angry at home, too.

"Is Jehran the little girl we ran into at the Museum of London?" asked Laura's mother.

Laura was startled. She thought of Jehran as older, with that sophisticated wardrobe, and worldly air, and the several languages she spoke. But to strangers, Jehran looked too young for high school. "Yes, that's the one."

"She reminded me of Billy," said Nicole. "Same coloring. Is it safe to go to her house?"

"Mom, she's the one who comes to school in her own bullet-proof limo."

"That makes me worry more, not less! Thomas, I don't want Laura hanging out with kids whose parents *know* there's going to be trouble!"

"Now, Nicole," said Laura's father. He telephoned Jehran's number and asked to speak to her father. Thomas discovered that for adult supervision of young girls, you could not beat an Arab household. There was probably no place in London, possibly the world, where girls were less likely to get in trouble.

"You know what Eddie said today?" said Laura. Here she was, actually close to terrorism, and all she wanted was for her parents to set the idea aside. When Eddie's words echoed in her brain, they sounded like blather—except when they sounded true and real.

"What?"

"He said when he grows up, he will participate in the destruction of Israel."

"In that student body, he's not the only one," said her father.

Laura braided her hair in front of her, watching the blond strands turn into a rope. "Do you think," said Laura, "that Billy—well, that Eddie—well—"

"No," said her mother. "I don't. Eddie is a jerk. It took intelligence and planning to kill Billy, and Eddie can hardly get on a bus. Anyway, he was on the bus with you when it happened. If Eddie was involved, he paid someone else to do it. Why would he do that?"

How sturdy her mother sounded. What a relief to hear that certain-sure tone again.

"Besides," said her father, "I can't place Israel in this. We're not Jews, we're not Israeli. If it's part of a plan to destroy Israel, why Billy?"

"That's the whole problem," said Laura. "Everything I come up with, Billy *doesn't* fit into."

Her parents nodded. "I could get through the days better," said Nicole, "if we knew why. I don't want it to be random. I don't want it to mean nothing."

But they were drawing closer to the conclusion that Billy's death meant nothing.

Oh please, thought Laura that night, trying to sleep. Please don't let Billy's death be nothing. Please let there be something. Something in life, something in death, something in God . . .

Something.

Jehran lived on a "crescent," a pretty British word for a short private street. Tall black iron fences rimmed front gardens. The tips of the fences were gold, like spears dipped in molten blood.

A soldier opened Jehran's door as Laura came up the walk. His olive drab was decorated with ribbons and medals, as if he had just finished up a little war. He had too much mustache. A drooping mustache always seemed threatening to Laura.

Jehran's downstairs was painted concert-hall red,

and it was large enough to be one. Persian rugs in explosive colors were strewn about in layers. There were several sofas in the same dark blue velvet on which jewelry stores place diamonds. Yet the sitting room was barren, like a motel.

This is not a home, thought Laura. They lease the paintings and the grand piano until they go to another haven: South America or Canada. They are not burdened with possessions. They have only bank accounts.

Jehran, smiling from a balcony, waved her guests up to her suite. Behind the stairs, Laura caught a glimpse of several uniformed men standing at the far end of a wide hall. They were silent and unmoving, like a mural.

The house had an *army* living in it.

Laura was sick with wishing she had stayed home. The world was spinning off in too many directions. Laura was falling behind in class. She was obsessed with her friends' histories; she was not sleeping. The real slumber party rule was laughter. Laura did not know how to laugh anymore.

It was a relief to reach Jehran's room The colors here were beautiful, like ripe fruit. Deep peach, apricot, and plum. Dark wood gleamed and curved in corners.

Jehran's bed was enormous. In America, beds were predictable: twin, double, queen, king. In Europe, they could be any old size (not that this massive bed could be termed "any old size"; if the largest American bed was king, this was emperor).

Laura could not imagine lying on that bed on her

stomach, listening to some tame Brit rock station with an Australian DJ.

"Is your mother home, Jehran?" asked Con.

Jehran shook her head. "My mother died many years ago. So did my father. I live with my oldest brother."

"I'm so sorry, Jehran," said Con. "That's awful! I didn't know."

"It's ancient history," said Jehran courteously. "I never think of it anymore."

"How old is your brother?" Bethany asked.

I don't have a brother! thought Laura, as shocked as if she had not had a month to realize this. When a stranger asks about my family, do I say I'm an only child? Do I say I had a brother once?

"He's twenty-six years older than I am," said Jehran.

"Your brother?"

"There were brothers and sisters in between," said Jehran, "but they did not survive."

Laura was horrified. She was not getting through life with *one* dead brother. There was no way she could stay at this awful party. Could she bail out after supper? Of course, Middle Easterners didn't even think about dinner till nine or ten. By ten o'clock at Laura's, they were ready for bed, or at least yelling at Billy to clean up his mess before bedtime, since Billy made a mess wherever he breathed.

She kept forgetting Billy didn't breathe. How long would it take to know that Billy was dead? To know it completely; the way you knew the Atlantic Ocean was on the right, and the Pacific was on the left and America was in the middle?

Snacks appeared. Food was usually a good diversion, but here it was brought by an elderly servant robed in floor-length black. The fabric was coarse and there was enough for a tent. The woman struggled with heavy trays. Her hands were swollen, fingers knotted with age.

Con tried to help, but this just upset the old woman, so the girls looked away and hoped this would end quickly.

There were several kinds of olives, salads in all colors and textures, bowls of yogurt, dishes of toasted nuts, and hummus for dip. The bread was soft, as thin and round as a doily. Jehran showed them how to rip off a leaf and scoop up hummus.

Laura could not eat. She hoped Jehran would forget her plan to lift Laura's spirits. Laura didn't think she even had a spirit right now.

Clearly, discussion of Jehran's family was not the stuff of which successful slumber parties are made. Con, taking on the role of hostess, turned to Tiffany, who could be counted upon to think of herself as interesting. "Where are you from, Tiff?" asked Con brightly, as if she cared. "What brought you to London?"

"We're from Boston. We're Irish. My father is very involved with the Cause. He raises money. But my mother thought this school would be better and safer, so we're living here and he goes back and forth. America, Ireland, England, all the time, back and forth."

"Cause?" said Laura, recognizing a buzzword.

"Even *you* must know, Laura," said Tiffany, "that the English have held Northern Ireland prisoner for generations. Their army occupies our land. They keep our people from getting jobs. Whenever there's trouble, it's their fault."

"That's ridiculous," said Bethany, "you're such a jerk, Tiffany. England is doing the best it can to bring peace to Northern Ireland. And my father says there wouldn't *be* Troubles if it weren't for dumb Americans sending money."

Yes, even Laura knew by now that all over the world, people were elbowing and shooting and hating. Everyone was convinced, like Tiffany, that if the other guy would just move to the next block, or across the river, or into the next nation, life would be good at last.

Here she was, among friends at a slumber party, and they were this quick to fight. "So, Tiff," said Laura, "what's your father raise money for? Bombs?"

"Oh shut up, Laura," said Tiff. "*We* are not the terrorists. *They* are."

Eight girls tried to think of a way to get off this subject for good, but Tiffany stomped right over them. "I know what you really want, Laura. You want Billy's death to have meaning. You want to find out that your brother died for freedom, or some grand cause."

Laura hated Tiffany. She hated the word "Cause." What value did any Cause have, if it made people murder each other? "Billy didn't have causes! He had collections. Anyway, Billy could never stop talking. If he'd had a cause, he'd have told everybody. Billy never kept a secret in his life. He was one big explosion."

This was grotesquely true.

Con took over. "My, Jehran, what a huge dressing room you have! May we try your perfumes?"

Jehran looked startled, so Bethany said, "Key slumber party activity, Jehran, using up the hostess's perfume."

The girls drifted through the suite, admiring and touching. They explored scents and lotions and intriguing bottles. Only Jehran and Laura were still on the emperor bed. Jehran sat cross-legged, so small and light that the huge mattress hardly sank around her.

"Laura?" The word was hardly audible. Laura felt it instead, like Braille on her cheek. Jehran moved closer. Her face was strangely white beneath her olive skin, as if her soul had fallen out, and there was nothing behind those dark features. Laura pressed back against the pillows.

Jehran rested a finger on her lips, the universal gesture for silence, and nodded slightly toward the dressing room. "I must share a secret with you," whispered Jehran.

Laura did not want Jehran's secrets. Twenty-six years of brothers and sisters dead? This scary house

with its rented magnificence? An army lounging downstairs while young girls frolicked upstairs? A pathetic
old woman staggering upstairs in her black Arabic
robes?

Jehran's heavy hair fell against Laura's face. The
hair was cold, and then the room was cold. Laura was
afraid.

Jehran whispered, "I need you, Laura."

Laura could not imagine Jehran needing her.

"Laura," said Jehran, "you *can* give meaning to
Billy's death."

If only that could be true.

"Let me use his passport," said Jehran.

CHAPTER 10

Billy's passport. So meaningless back home.

So essential abroad.

"It would honor Billy," whispered Jehran. "It would give his death a purpose."

Honor. The word sounded proud and strong, and Laura thought of her brother, brave enough to hug that bomb to his chest instead of throwing it into the crowd to save himself. A chest where medals should hang, but that instead had been blown to pieces.

Purpose. Death. Honor. Laura could not connect these words to *passport.*

"But why?" Laura whispered back. She felt threatened.

Con, Kyrene, Bethany, Samira, and Tiffany sloshed perfume around. Their giggles were background music.

"My life is in danger, Laura."

How foolish the sentence sounded. This was a slumber party. Nobody's life was in danger; only the contents of the perfume bottles were in danger. Then Laura turned back into a person whose brother had been murdered. It was true. A life could be in danger.

"I must flee this country," said Jehran, "and I have little time."

Danger required flight. Had not dozens of students fled L.I.A. when Billy was killed? And now it was Jehran's turn to flee. *Using Billy's passport?* It was creepy and ghastly. Laura did not want any part of this.

"I look like Billy," breathed Jehran. "Airport officials would believe that I am Billy Williams."

Jehran did look like Billy. Billy's own mother had noticed the resemblance. And beneath her elegant wardrobe, Jehran had the twiggy shape of a sixth-grade boy.

Billy's passport.

His vital statistics. No longer vital, for Billy no longer lived.

Vital only to Jehran.

In most countries, it was illegal to travel without identification, the way in America it was illegal to drive without your license. In all countries, it was impossible to leave without your passport.

In the dressing room, the knot of girls shrieked with laughter. "Jehran, this room is too much!" called Kyrene. "We just found your stash of emeralds!"

"Those are fake," called Jehran. "We don't keep the real jewels here. Wear them if you want."

Laura could well believe that the real jewels were

not here. Nothing here was real; it was a front Jehran must abandon for some dread reason.

How Billy would have loved it.

Escape! Flight! Chase! Danger!

On *his* passport.

Not even getting Kraft to agree to a macaroni franchise, not even finding out that the 007's of Britain were working on his case, would have pleased Billy more. He, secretly, clandestinely, would bring a friend to safety across the sea.

But it certainly wasn't legal. She could not imagine her mother and father saying yes. Laura wasn't sure she could say yes. There was something huge and awful about it, even though the passport itself was a slender pamphlet of a document.

Jehran's voice was thready. She was afraid of being overheard. Laura's spine turned to ice. Could those men with their heavy mustaches be listening?

"My brother," explained Jehran, "wants to go home. He wants home more than anything on earth. He is so unhappy in England."

Laura could understand that. Living in somebody else's world would be exhausting, year in and year out. *Laura* was exhausted and she was practically English herself; it was just plain hard to live in another country.

"But going home," said Jehran, "is possible only if my brother can make peace with the government. Otherwise he will be shot when he crosses the border.

Shot like the rest of our family. My father and my brothers. My mother and my sisters."

Laura, who had spent weeks imagining the impact of a bomb, thought of bullets instead.

"It is I who possess the family fortune," said Jehran. "We have great wealth, and it is mine. Many are the men who would like such wealth. So my brother has chosen a husband for me."

That sounded reasonable. Jehran's brother wouldn't let her marry some American from Massachusetts who'd take her home to be a Congregationalist like Laura.

"That man, my husband-to-be, will guarantee my brother's safety so he can return home after I am wed."

Laura was totally confused. The last thing Jehran would want under those circumstances was an American passport. Besides, she'd be going home to get married. What was so bad about that?

"This will happen in January," said Jehran. "I will not yet be sixteen. The man chosen for me is a general in his fifties. I will be his third wife. His is a traditional household. I will be forced to wear a black robe like my servant, and have my face covered by a solid veil with eye slits. I will not be permitted to leave my house. I will not be allowed books to read or television to watch or a radio to listen to. Laura, you are too American to know what such a marriage means. It is living death."

Laura had begun to see death: the shape of Billy gone. What was living death?

"My money would be his, and I would never be permitted to touch it. I would obey my husband, always, no matter how painful or cruel or wrong. I would have no purpose except to give birth to sons. If I had daughters, he would punish me and quickly get me pregnant again."

Laura felt as if Jehran occupied another planet, a place without gravity or sunrise. Perhaps if this arranged marriage occurred, it would be another planet, as strange and terrible as life without sunrise.

Jehran clutched Laura, her thin child's fingers biting into the flesh. "Trapped for life, Laura! Till I am buried."

Laura had just buried someone. It was so dark, being buried. She tried to think her way through this awful picture Jehran was drawing. "Is he . . . well . . . nice? Your fiancé?"

Jehran lost her composure. Her voice hit each syllable like sticks on the rim of a snare drum. "It isn't like that, Laura; don't be so American! He's fifty-four. He has other wives. He's tired of them, and he wants a young beautiful girl with a huge dowry."

Fifty-four. A decade older than Laura's father. Almost two decades older than her mother.

"I must leave England, Laura. Before my brother can seal this marriage, I must get out! Hide myself inside another life, inside a safer country: America. I have the money, but not the papers. Billy's passport would set me free."

The heavy draperies and tapestries of the room closed in on them, like the life Jehran wanted to flee.

Kyrene, Bethany, and Con flung themselves on the bed with Laura and Jehran. "I have a new career goal," said Kyrene, waving toward the dressing rooms. "I want to live like this."

Laura was trembling. She used the pillows to hide her face. So she had been right that the sullen soldiers downstairs were threatening. But not to Laura. They were keeping Jehran until they could purchase their way home with her money.

"Shove over," said Tiffany, squishing in. They shoved over.

"Shove over," said Samira. They shoved over to make room for Samira. Now it was a slumber party.

"Who here is going with the London Walk Club to Scotland after Christmas?" said Con.

"My family won't be here, of course," said Kyrene. "We're going to Vienna for Christmas."

"Show-off," said Con.

"We won't be here either, of course. We're going to Morocco," said Samira, "because it's warm and we're dying of sun deprivation."

"Well, I'm going," said Con.

"What are you talking about?" asked Jehran.

Laura's brain was exploding, trying to figure out how Jehran intended to use Billy's passport. But Jehran, who was in danger, calmly discussed the

London Walk Club program. Jehran must be used to hiding her feelings.

"The London Walk Club is taking the train for a change," said Con. "December twenty-eighth through the thirtieth, Mr. Hollober's taking us to Edinburgh."

"Nobody cares about the London Walk Club," said Tiffany. "Nobody has ever cared about the London Walk Club. Now, Jehran, the next thing you do at slumber parties is, you tell scary stories. Green monsters and creaking doors."

"Maniacs on the loose," agreed Bethany, "breaking windows in the black of night."

The girls giggled happily.

"Vampires lurking in closets that lead to hell," said Kyrene. "I will tell the secret story of the London vampire."

In marriage, Jehran would dress like a vampire. A black shroud with eye slits. Nobody except her husband would ever see her skin. The husband who was forty years older. Who already had wives. The wives were alive. They lived there. Laura did not like to think of the logistics of their bedrooms.

She could not understand the brother forcing a bad marriage on his sister, but Laura did understand wanting to go home.

Home was your same old neighborhood, and your same old trees at the same time of year, and your same old holidays, and your same old school building. Home was the comfort of things staying the way they were.

Jehran had arranged herself romantically against the pillows, her wonderful hair strewn around her. She'd have to cut her hair, thought Laura, to match Billy's passport photo. And she'd have to wear jeans.

She could not imagine Jehran in jeans.

Laura curled into a ball, the metallic threads of the bedspread pressed into her cheek, leaving an Islamic pattern.

Islam.

You thought that religion was a pact between you and God, but it wasn't. Religion was a group, and sometimes even a government. In some countries, religion was government by the tough and the cruel. Men who hated women. Men who wanted women literally locked in their clothes and their houses.

Laura would go home one day, to all that home meant, but Jehran was praying for the reverse: *Please, God, never make me go home.*

And only Laura Williams could make it come true.

The passports, thought Laura, are in Daddy's bottom desk drawer. I suppose I could slip Billy's into my book bag and hand it to Jehran at lunch on Monday. But—

She was suddenly terrified for Jehran, facing the world alone, completely and forever alone. What if she, Laura, had had to come to England by herself? At fifteen? Gotten off the plane at Heathrow alone? No parent. No grown-up. No friend.

What if she had to find a place to live, pay for it, figure out how to get groceries and how to cook them, and how to do laundry, and how to tell lies, hundreds of lies, lies she would have to remember forever, and never get wrong?

Suppose Jehran landed at Kennedy Airport in New York. Jehran and thousands of other immigrants. Nobody would know Jehran was immigrating, of course. They would think she was eleven years old, a boy named Billy Williams going home to visit relatives, and—

And there was a problem.

Airplanes didn't let eleven-year-olds travel alone. An unaccompanied minor had to be brought to the airport, where a grown-up would fill out forms and put the kid's hand in the hand of the airline personnel. At the other end, the flight attendants did not just let the kid get off the plane either. The grown-up named in the paperwork had to show up.

So Jehran couldn't just buy a ticket and get on a plane as Billy.

There had to be an adult in the escape.

But who?

Jehran's adult—her brother—would never let her go. That was the point.

And Laura's adults—her mother and father—would never cooperate. They would say Jehran's brother knew best, and the Williamses could not interfere in a private family decision, *and they would never let Laura give away Billy's passport.*

CHAPTER

11

There were no decent desserts for lunch on Monday. The cafeteria staff actually thought Rich Tea Biscuits qualified as dessert.

"Rich Tea Biscuits taste like Animal Crackers," said Con, "but they're not as much fun to eat."

"Are you a head biter?" asked Jimmy.

"No," said Con. "If you eat their heads first, how are they going to feel pain when you eat the rest of them?"

The Americans laughed. Laura enjoyed keeping Americanisms to herself, but Con had no selfish side and described Animal Cracker boxes with their little shoestrings.

"I have to put some lipstick on," said Laura. She pushed her chair back and wandered out of the cafeteria.

Con was mildly surprised. She didn't remember Laura wearing lipstick, or needing to restore it after lunch.

Jehran's choice to fix her lipstick surprised nobody, because Jehran was always perfect—hair flawless, scarf hanging just so, jewels glittering. Con paid no attention to Jehran.

Mohammed paid attention to Jehran. And he paid attention to Samira, who was glaring at Jehran's back.

The girls' room was relatively large and met U.S. standards for handicapped access. Nobody at L.I.A. had a wheelchair, so Laura and Jehran slid together into the extra-large stall.

Jehran gave Laura a fat square English envelope of thin brown paper. Laura opened it to find a thick stack of English pounds. Her jaw dropped. It was a huge amount of cash.

"You must buy the airplane ticket for me," Jehran mouthed.

Laura was not ready to think about buying tickets. She had not even come to the final decision to take Billy's passport. Yes, it would be a good thing for Jehran. But was it a good thing for Billy? For her mother? For her father?

Laura needed time to think.

"I will go to New York," Jehran whispered. "In New York, I will be surrounded by other foreigners. New York will be like London. Everybody else is a foreigner, too. And in New York, my English accent will help me, because Americans love English accents."

This was true, and Jehran's accent made Americans think of castles and princesses.

"All by yourself, though!" protested Laura. Even to Laura, New York on your own sounded scary. But for an Arab girl traveling under a false passport?

"That's what immigrants to New York have always done," Jehran pointed out. "Remember the immigration unit in American history?"

London International Academy offered a year of American history because you couldn't graduate from an American high school without it. Laura expected only American kids needing the credit would take it, but the class was full of foreigners. Laura was surprised that Jehran had taken it.

"Italian and Polish and Irish and German immigrants!" Jehran whispered excitedly. "They were children when they crossed the Atlantic. If they could do it, I can do it."

When Laura studied immigration, it seemed to her that every immigrant was a thirteen-year-old sailing steerage on some hideous boat who, twenty-five years later, had become a millionaire and coached Little League.

But it didn't matter, because Jehran couldn't travel as an eleven-year-old by herself—or himself, if she were Billy. Laura outlined the problem.

Jehran shrugged. "You'll have to come with me, then."

"Come with you?"

"Sssssshh!"

"What are you talking about, Jehran? I can't just get on a plane and fly back to America. My mother and father would never agree to that."

"You won't ask them. You'll just come. When we land in New York, you'll turn around and take the very next flight back to England. You won't be gone twenty-four hours."

"Impossible," said Laura.

"This will be better, anyway," said Jehran. "You'll be my big sister, Laura, and you're sixteen, so you'll be my adult. I won't be an unaccompanied minor, and there will be no paperwork. Besides, when I'm pretending to be Billy, my British accent would betray me. They'd know I'm not a boy from Massachusetts. This way, you will do the talking."

"Jehran, it won't work. My parents would never let us do it."

Jehran was too excited to allow problems. "With this cash, you will buy us both tickets. Then all I have to do is get out of my house and away from my brother. I am confident I can accomplish that. With you, Laura, I can land in America without having to answer questions!"

That was what crossing a border was all about.

Questions.

You'd show your passport in England, and go through the electronic weapons-search gate, and now show both your plane ticket and your passport, and then do it again before actually boarding the plane.

At landing, you had to tell what you'd been doing

abroad. Business travel? Vacation? What were your reasons? How much money were you bringing?

Everywhere in airports were doors and guards and gates to ensure that only authorized people moved on.

"Come back to earth, Jehran," said Laura. "How could I be away from home for twenty-four hours? What would I tell my parents?"

Jehran brushed this away with a flip of her scarf. "American girls are allowed to do anything. You have no morals."

"If that's what you think of Americans, go to Brazil!"

The bathroom door opened. Girls swarmed in, shrieking and giggling. Doors slammed, makeup was shared. It was enough noise so that the whispering could continue.

Laura planned to call Jehran names, and end their friendship, and never speak to her again, but Jehran began to cry. "I'm so sorry, Laura. I didn't mean to hurt your feelings. I have great respect for American families." The tears silvered her cheeks.

How quickly I was going to abandon her, thought Laura, ashamed. "Don't you see, Jehran, if I were gone twenty-four hours, my parents wouldn't just telephone Mr. Evans. They'd telephone every police department in England. In Europe! In the world!" In fact, thought Laura, they would be scared to death. Could such a thing really happen? Could fear for Laura explode in her mother's face as the bomb had exploded in Billy's, and kill her mother?

"You cannot let me down," begged Jehran. "Laura, I have nobody else to ask. Any day, my brother may say it has been arranged, and I am to leave. I will beg him to let me finish the school year, but a woman does not require education, so that will not matter."

But Laura could not vanish overnight. And no girlfriend, certainly not Con, would support her in a lie that involved an overnight absence. She started to hand the package of money back, but Jehran held up her hand, and her eyes were fire, sending off sparks. "I know what we can do!" breathed Jehran.

Laura didn't.

"The London Walk Club," said Jehran. "We'll pretend we're going to Edinburgh."

Regardless of Laura's emotions toward Mr. Hollober, she had been forced to continue attending current events. She made a point of not listening, and then remembered she was trying to be less ignorant, so she listened after all. She made sure her hostile attitude stayed on her face for Mr. Hollober to see.

Mr. Hollober discussed social customs around the world. In what country, and why, did people shake hands instead of bowing? In what country, and why, did well-to-do females wear ragged torn clothes (America) or drape cloth over their noses (Saudi Arabia)?

Laura tuned in.

"If a girl from an observant Moslem family were to

fall in love with a Christian," said Mr. Hollober, "or flirt, or expose her face or limbs or hair in front of men except her father and brothers, she would taint her family's honor. She would be punished because honor of the family matters more than she does."

"What kind of punishment?" said Tiffany.

Mr. Hollober said the family might shoot her.

"Come on," said Tiffany, not believing a word of that.

Mr. Hollober insisted he was telling the truth. "Girls who tempt men are criminals. Girls who disobey their fathers and brothers are criminals. And criminals in Islamic countries pay with their lives."

So if Jehran disobeyed her brother, he would not yell at her. He would execute her.

Laura kept her shudder inside. Trapping the shudder nauseated her. She was afraid of throwing up.

"Some of us," said Samira, "feel this shows great love from our families. Our families *care* what we do, as opposed to American families, who don't care what their daughters do."

"You wanna get shot for falling in love?" said Tiffany.

"I will marry the husband my parents choose," said Samira. "Love will come afterward."

"Mohammed," said Tiffany, "is that true? You know any situations like that? Guys who shoot their sisters and it isn't murder, it's civic duty?"

"Tiffany," said Con, "try to be civilized, okay?"

"Watch who you're accusing of being uncivilized," said Tiffany. "I wanna know, then, Samira, what you're doing in a Western school, where kids date, and some of them sleep around, and some of them do drugs, and some of them drink and swear? How come your loving family lets you in the door of a sick place like this?"

Laura thought that was a good question—it certainly applied to Jehran—but Mr. Hollober joined Con's team, which never answered difficult questions, or better yet, didn't allow anybody to ask them. This was called diplomacy.

They were wrong when they said if you went overseas, you would better understand other nations and people and religions. The more Laura heard, the less she understood. The less she wanted to understand. She usually wanted to give American lessons so people would see that the American way was best.

But even Laura knew that you never said that out loud. Not in an international school. Not if you wanted to live.

Billy had said everything out loud. And everybody had reacted like the Jamaican bus driver: they liked him, anyhow.

She was no closer to Billy's killer. There was no real way to get closer. Would it give his death meaning to use his passport? If Laura said no, and Jehran had to obey her brother, she would have a terrible life, a life she did not choose. But if Laura said yes, and Jehran tried to escape and got caught—she would not have a life.

o   o   o

Laura's mother was studying Billy's chair.

The table sat four. It would look funny without his chair. But she could not bear the sight of the chair Billy liked to tip backward, and she would have to yell at him not to do that, and he would say, "Mom, have you ever actually known a person who fell backward and cracked his skull? It's a myth, like alligators in the sewers of New York. Real people can balance their chairs on two legs."

She put her hands on the top slat of the chair back, to shift it out of sight, but she thought: if I take away the chair, how can Billy have supper with us again?

Then she thought: he's not going to. You know he's not. There is no resurrection in this world.

She could not move the chair. It would always be Billy's, and would always be empty. She staggered away from it.

Nicole found the kitchen on the first try. It looked alien, the way it had the day they arrived in London, and nothing about the kitchen was shaped, or opened, or worked, the way it did back home.

Nicole remembered the first time she did dishes. It felt weird. You didn't go to London to do dishes. You went to London to see Windsor Castle or catch a glimpse of the royal family.

BBC Radio played a cathedral choir. Thin melancholy Christmas music.

Nicole Williams could not believe that a mother was expected to face Christmas without her child.

Christmas, the holiday of giving.

Children aren't old enough to give, thought Nicole. They take. Taking is the beginning of love. Nobody ever received as joyfully as Billy. And I can give him nothing now. Not one toy. Not one more minute on earth.

At the end of the day, Nicole was still in the kitchen, staring at the cans of SpaghettiOs that were still waiting for Billy.

Con trapped Laura at their lockers. "I asked my father," said Con, "about your idea that terrorists are country specific. I said could you really get a good combination of person and country and religion, and zero in on your terrorist?"

Con's father might actually know things like that, so Laura listened.

"Dad says Libya, Syria, Iran, and Iraq are the biggies in terrorism. I told him you were going for Northern Ireland, but he pooh-poohed that. The Irish raise so much money in America, they're not about to murder a sweet little American kid."

Laura was hard inside, waiting, needing the fact that would take her forward.

"You're imagining a conspiracy," Con said. "You're picturing a whole country and spies and bombers and

demented expatriates gathering together to extermi-
nate Billy. But there's no logic to that."

"Where is the logic?" Laura tried to dial the combination on her lock.

"My father says terrorists are plain old bad guys.
Instead of expecting them to be brilliant and complex,
you should go for the quick and ugly."

"Oh, Con, that's stupid. That's just another dial-a-
horoscope answer! *Today you will find something ugly.*
Leave me alone, Con."

Laura walked away without getting what she needed
from the locker, sick of her best friend, sick of all
friends and friendly things. Laura could not bear the
possibility of talking to anybody else. Jimmy, Kyrene,
Mohammed, Tiffany, Andrew, Bethany—she could not
stand the sight or the sound of them. As for waiting on
the corner with Eddie, she would never do that again.

Laura crossed the street instead. When she glanced
back at the school, she saw Mohammed. From so far
away, she could not tell that he was handsome, only
that he stood very still and stared back. Next to the
holly trees was Andrew. How American he seemed,
team jacket hanging open, huge expensive sneakers
untied. Jimmy was waving to her, and his wave seemed
to curl, as if summoning her. Con had pressed herself
against the side of the building, head low, pretending
she was not there, but looking at Laura from beneath
her falling hair.

Why were they looking at her?

Didn't they have anything better to do?

Laura strode down the block as if she had plans, and it began to pour, which she should have known it would do, but she still wasn't conditioned to England's constant rain. She had no umbrella.

A few blocks away lay Regent's Park.

Regent's Park was much bigger than the Boston Common Laura knew. On sunny days, there were soccer balls and Frisbees, black children and white children, dogs on leashes, and many more dogs not on leashes. Even today, in such cold, sloppy weather, there were two soccer games.

A sense of evil enveloped Laura. The sum of her thoughts was dark glass behind which anything could hide: Billy, the escalator, the police, Mr. Evans, the mumbled funeral in a strange church, the stares of sixth graders, the vanishing of classmates, the anger of Mr. Frankel, the horror of Eddie, the awful situation of Jehran, and the awful thing that Jehran wanted from Laura.

And eyes, eyes everywhere.

She was being followed.

She jerked behind a closed-for-winter restaurant, ducked around a thick hedge, and waited.

But nobody came.

And when she edged out, no one was there.

Oh you terrorist! thought Laura Williams. What have you done to me? All my friends have to do is stand on a corner and I'm afraid of them.

o   o   o

Con Vikary's father was picking her up at school because she had a dentist appointment. Con huddled beneath an overhang to stay dry, and she could see Andrew and Mohammed and Eddie watching Laura. Con tried to brush off Laura yelling at her, but she couldn't. It hurt.

Con moved every year. It was so hard to make friends! And she had to make them continually, in different countries, and if she had to find another best friend only halfway into the year . . . Con felt weak and lonely and awful.

"We're all watching Laura, aren't we?" said Jimmy Hopkins.

She jumped a foot. "You scared me, Jimmy."

"We're terrorist bombing groupies. Laura is drama and tragedy and we want to be part of the action."

"That's sick, Jimmy." Con was so relieved when her father pulled up. She didn't look back at Jimmy and she didn't look over at Mohammed and Andrew.

Dad kissed her. "Have a good day, Con?"

There seemed no way to talk about the kind of day she had had. Con was beginning to fear that she would always mean well, and always screw up. "Daddy, let's not go to the dentist. Let's go to the patisserie."

Her father grinned at her, and his grin was so normal, so American, that she felt safe for a minute, and she was surprised. I didn't know I felt unsafe.

But after Billy, we're all unsafe.

Forever.

It was a hike across Regent's Park, but eventually Laura would come out close to Heathfold Gardens. The wind felt as if it had come from the Siberian steppes, but the soccer teams kept playing, bare legs in icy mud. Laura trudged on. The thin tower of the mosque rose above the treetops, and the cages of the London Zoo were half visible beyond the playground.

At last she was on Finchley Road. A service at the mosque had just ended. The worshippers were distinctive: bold African prints, delicate Indian elegance, and the tentlike black envelopes of rule-abiding Middle Eastern women. Laura wondered if she would have anything to say to such women, or they to her.

What would it be like to spend your life inside a black robe?

What would it be like to know that people were serious about the word "obey"—that yes, you were going to obey your husband every day of your life in every word he said?

Once she had asked Samira if she went to that mosque.

"I've never gone to a mosque," Samira had said.

Laura knew you could be Christian and not pay attention to church, but she had not known you could be Islamic and not pay attention to the mosque.

There, on the sidewalk, stood Mr. Evans, smoking a cigarette in the rain. "Laura," he said. It was a lecture in one word. "You're soaked. Here. I'll take you to tea. We'll go to Louis' Patisserie—it isn't far—you'll dry out and they do quite a nice tea there."

Afternoon tea was the best thing about London.

Basically, tea meant a really good after-school snack. They brought you a pot of tea, milk in little pitchers, and sugar in fat brown lumps that were lumpy, not the square squares of American sugar lumps.

Then you ordered your pastry. London was pastry heaven. "Sweets," they were called, or hideously, "pudds." This was short for pudding, which sounded thick and blobby, but nobody meant pudding; they meant dessert.

How disgusted Billy had been to learn that British children had mostly lost interest in tea. "Where do your kids go for after-school snacks?" he had asked his father's British colleagues.

"McDonald's," they told him.

Billy was absolutely totally disgusted with British children. "How are you supposed to get to know other people's cultures," he said darkly, "when they keep trading them in?"

Laura was better now at handling Billy memories. She said to Mr. Evans, "I'm having tea with you only if you skip the lecture."

"Mmmm," said Mr. Evans. "I'm afraid I cannot skip it, Laura. There's a bit to discuss." He popped her into a car driven by a policeman whose expression indicated that he had better stuff to do than drive Laura around. Or else he had appendicitis.

The tables at Louis' were very tiny. Laura and Mr. Evans were jammed in among strangers. Laura chose a Hungarian pastry, with lots of layers, and cinnamon, and raisins and butter. The sweet hot milky taste of her tea was like childhood: like the warmth of home before bad things happened.

Mr. Evans was very serious about his pastry choice. Laura liked a person to whom food mattered. Billy, of course, had been extremely serious about his desserts. He usually ordered something with clotted cream, which tasted like whipped cream, but more so.

Mr. Evans got butter on the sleeve of his too-large wool jacket and Laura knew she could tell him Jehran's problem. He would help solve it, and that way she wouldn't have to—

"Laura," said Mr. Evans, "you and your family need to go back to the States. It's hard on you to be here, and it's especially hard on your mother. Christmas is coming, and you should be home. You could pressure your family to return to Boston."

"We have a right to stay, Mr. Evans," said Laura, who had no idea whether they had any such right. Perhaps the British would deport the Williamses. She almost grinned. Billy would be awfully sorry to miss getting deported.

If we go home, she thought, how can I help Jehran?

She had forgotten the fat pack of money. Her eyes flew open and her hand flew to her purse, to be sure she hadn't lost it. She wet her lips.

Suddenly, queerly, she was afraid of Mr. Evans. Of what he could do to her, and to Jehran. All this money. Was it Jehran's? Was it stolen? Would Mr. Evans arrest Laura if he found it? And the passport—if Laura told, Mr. Evans could confiscate the precious passport that had been Billy's.

"But is it best for your family?" said Mr. Evans. "Laura, I have the sense that your parents are staying so your school year isn't disrupted. But it has been disrupted. And you'd be better off at home."

"You just don't want me talking to people," said Laura. Who had complained. Jimmy? Mohammed? Samira? Con?

"What do you think you will accomplish?" said Mr. Evans nicely, as if he really wanted to know.

Laura wasn't accomplishing a thing. She might as well have been playing football by sitting in a chair. She couldn't score because she didn't even know who the enemy team was. "I have to try, Mr. Evans."

"No," said Mr. Evans. "There are plenty of people trying, Laura. They are experts. They know what they're doing."

"If they knew what they were doing, they'd have done it."

Mr. Evans gave Laura the well-known *American teens are so rude* look. "You are losing friends, Laura. Treading on toes."

"It isn't a question of *toes*," said Laura, shotgun angry. "It's a question of *bombs*. Bombs that splatter you so you don't have a heart or arms or legs, never mind toes."

Her voice had skyrocketed.

People were staring.

The pianist, who had been taking a break, went quickly back to the keyboard.

She had no use for Mr. Evans, none at all. Toes! As if her brother's murder were no more than a day that hadn't gone well.

Mr. Evans gave Laura her instructions for future behavior.

The usual rules, thought Laura, for those of us whose brothers get blown up. *Don't get into a car without checking the backseat for crouching murderers. Don't leave your suitcase unattended. Don't accept packages from strangers.*

In her purse lay a package she had accepted from a stranger.

CHAPTER 12

Laura was careful.

When school ended, she waited until her friends had left by car, or bus, or Underground, and then she took a bus as if to go shopping at Selfridges. After a block or so, she got off and took a different bus, walked the wrong way down a one-way street, and entered the Underground at a station she never normally used.

She took a train to an area not for tourists: city-grim and city-sad. It reminded Laura of slummy corners of Boston, though the architecture, and certainly the speech, was different. Trash in the streets, abandoned cars where grass should have grown, sullen children smoking in doorways.

I wouldn't set foot in this neighborhood at home! she thought. Why am I doing this in London?

Again she felt eyes on her back, but these were not

the eyes of friends; they were the eyes of strangers, deciding what kind of victim she would make.

A stupid one, thought Laura Williams, walking swiftly past betting shops, pubs, and abandoned stores.

Within a block she found a cut-rate travel agency, as she had known she would. London was full of tourists and immigrants and aliens and strangers, and all of them came from somewhere and would want to go back one day.

Travel posters inside the windows of the shop had faded, and the tape holding them down was brown and split. Brochures curled at the corners. When she entered, the floor was filthy with squashed-out cigarettes and the air was gray. The travel agent was Indian, overweight and irritated, talking through a cigarette that bounced between his thin lips.

What was she doing? Why had she not chosen a nice travel agency in a nice neighborhood? This was London! Millions of people! Nobody was going to recognize her, nobody knew her to start with.

"Two round-trip tickets to New York City, please," she said. "American Airlines. Departing December twenty-eighth." She used her most London accent, and he looked at her oddly, and she realized she had used her Jehran-*Masterpiece Theatre* voice, which nobody in this neighborhood possessed.

But she did not interest him. Only ticket sales interested him, and he went into his computer.

Laura forced herself to concentrate on the plan.

The London Walk Club was taking a morning train

to Edinburgh on December twenty-eighth. Laura and Jehran would fly out that morning, too, get to New York, Laura would escort Jehran to the taxi stand, and Jehran—brave, brave Jehran—would be on her own in a new world. Laura would turn around and fly back. Jehran would disappear without a trace.

If an official asked, Laura would say she and her little brother were visiting Grandma over vacation. But that meant Laura, who had to fly back the same day, could not display a return ticket for that day. Customs officials would want to know why a visit to Grandma was not at least for one night.

It wouldn't matter to Jehran, who would just toss her return ticket in the trash and vanish.

But Laura would have to have a second ticket to come home on. She had decided to buy this at another agency on another day.

The ticket agent had difficulty finding seats. Laura had forgotten how busy Christmas season was. Seats were sold. Oh no! she thought, it's not going to work!

"No seats on American," said the man. "Would you travel British Air?"

If she had not lived in London for months, she would not have understood a single word. The accent combination of immigrant from India and slum London was another whole language. "Well, okay," said Laura, forgetting to sound Brit.

He paid no attention, but typed. At last came the welcome sound of the printer spitting out tickets.

She handed him pound notes, the equivalent of hundreds and hundreds of dollars. The man's expression sharpened, and he tried to see how much more cash she was carrying. She read the tickets carefully to see that they were the right times and dates. Williams, L. seemed acceptable, printed out on the tickets, but Williams, W. looked wrong and terrible. She stuffed the tickets into her purse, tried to thank the man, but couldn't, tried to walk calmly out, but bumped into a man even fatter and more angry than the clerk, a man ready to yell at anybody, and Laura was there, and she bolted.

Up the scary street to the Underground she ran. She showed her commutation ticket and got on the next train without caring if it went where she needed to go.

The noisy rhythm of the train calmed her down.

She was not a brilliant strategist. She was a fool.

Jimmy Hopkins loved television detective shows where they followed the guy, but he had always wondered if it really worked.

It worked.

Following Laura was easy.

He hadn't planned to do it. But he couldn't help noticing that Laura did not leave school when everybody else did. He didn't go back inside to look for her. He just waited.

Twenty minutes after everybody else was gone, out came Laura, wearing an old raincoat and a navy scarf that were an excellent disguise; they made her old and boring, and he knew who it was only because he was looking for her.

Not only did she get on a bus that would not take her home, but she got off that bus at the very next stop—Jimmy could still see her way down the road. He raced after her, book bag whapping against his back, and caught up just as she was disappearing into an Underground station. At first he thought she didn't want to use the station where Billy got killed. But then she got on a train that wouldn't take her home either.

She's going shopping, he said to himself, or to Con's house, or running errands, or something.

But the raincoat made him curious.

And he'd wanted to follow somebody all his life.

So he followed.

Laura was a bundle of jitters, thinking of all she had to do and pretend to do. She had borrowed Con's tour guide and, as the train took her home, she read up on Edinburgh.

How do I fake Scotland? Mom and Dad will ask about it. And they'll meet the train; what do I do about the train? Do I show up at St. Pancras Station when the class returns from Edinburgh and pretend I was with them? Mr. Hollober won't let me get away with that. Besides, they'll be away two nights, and I'll be away one night. What do I do that other night? Pretend I took an earlier train from Edinburgh? Stay at a hotel?

Laura patted her tickets and her extra money. This had such a familiar feel that she realized she had been patting her purse constantly; she was one of those creepy people you kept your eye on in subways, wondering if they were about to go nuts and get violent.

She looked up.

She kept forgetting: this was London; nobody paid any attention to anybody here. People slept, read their papers, or stared at their feet.

She did not want to keep secrets from her parents. And when they did go home to Boston, and did need passports, and Billy's was not there . . . she'd have to tell them everything in the end, anyhow. Should she just tell them in the beginning?

After Jehran is safely in New York, Laura said to herself, I'll tell. Of course, they'll be mad at me, what parent wouldn't be? Flying back and forth across the Atlantic Ocean and lying that I was on a school trip?

Seriously mad.

But that won't be the problem.

The problem is: will they keep Jehran's secret?

Jimmy stared at sun-wrecked posters in a nasty little slum travel agency.

If Laura were going someplace with her family, first of all her parents would make the arrangements, and second of all they'd never ever use this shop. What was she up to? Jimmy wanted to know what she'd gone in the agency for.

He hesitated. He had never offered anybody a bribe.

Billy wouldn't have hesitated. Jimmy drew a deep breath, pretended he was Billy Williams, walked up to the travel agent, and set two ten-pound notes on the counter. "I need a printout of her travel plans," he said, pointing at the disappearing Laura.

There was silence. The man dangled his cigarette between his lips, and the smoke curled offensively.

Was Jimmy being laughed at? About to be arrested? Had he offered too little?

The printer clattered.

The Asian behind the counter neither smiled nor frowned, just sucked in smoke, handed him the printout, and took the twenty pounds.

Jimmy was a little chilled at how easy that was.

He walked out. He, too, went swiftly up the hill toward the Underground entrance. Too late to catch Laura, but plenty of time to get caught by some mugger.

He unfolded the printout.

Laura had purchased two round-trip tickets to Kennedy Airport in New York City: one for herself . . . and one for Billy.

The next day in the cafeteria, Mohammed managed to get in line behind Samira.

Jehran and Laura were already seated, heads together over macaroni and cheese. Samira shot a glance of loathing at the American girl.

"It is interesting," said Mohammed carefully, "that Laura and Jehran have become good friends." He would not have expected Jehran to include Americans at her party; she would consider them a stain on the carpets. However, he, too, had been touched by Jehran's concern for Laura.

Samira shrugged. "Laura is a fool and an American. I do not understand why Jehran is playing with her."

Mohammed could not deny that Laura was a fool and an American, but he was very fond of her. "Have you been friends with Jehran long?" he asked. "Did you attend that party?"

"The slumber party was strange."

"It sounds strange to me," admitted Mohammed. He could not think of a circumstance in which he would invite eight boys to sleep on the floor of his bedroom. It was an American custom that somehow did not sound American. According to Andrew, who knew these things, it was a girl's custom, not a boy's.

"Jehran was catering to the Americans. It made me angry. You know as well as I do that Jehran despises Americans. The whole reason she's in an international school is to get to know the enemy. I know she's giving information to her family."

Mohammed puzzled over this. What information? Con, whose father was important in the American

Embassy, might have interesting information if her father were the type to talk at the dinner table. But Mohammed could not imagine Con telling anybody her father's business.

Tiffany. Her parents were with an industrial carpet company, so what useful facts could Tiffany reveal to Jehran? Changes in industrial rug prices?

Samira didn't know and didn't care. She was just angry that an American was coming ahead of her in Jehran's affections.

Affections, thought Mohammed. Jehran is not an affectionate person. Laura is affectionate. But Jehran is calculating. What calculations does Jehran have that include Laura Williams?

Jimmy was mostly surprised by how normal Laura looked, separating the chocolate sides of Oreo cookies Bethany had brought to share and eating the filling first.

Okay, said Jimmy to himself. So what do I do? Laura thinks she can go home with her dead brother. She bought him a seat. She's planning to leave December twenty-eighth and stay for a week.

Okay. I could call her parents. So, *Hi, Mr. and Mrs. Williams, did you know that Laura has flipped?*

In Jimmy's opinion, Mrs. Williams was already over the edge. He hadn't met Mr. Williams, so he didn't know about the father, but Jimmy didn't want to make that call.

He could tell the headmaster. *So, Mr. Frankel, guess*

what Laura thinks she can do over vacation? Transport her brother's ghost to Kennedy.

He could tell his own parents.

But Jimmy felt a loyalty to Laura he could not define. Laura was nobody's girlfriend, certainly not his, and yet he felt very close to her, as if they had shared something special.

He didn't want to betray her.

Since Laura could *not* take Billy to New York on December twenty-eighth, the most likely thing to happen was that Laura would wake up realizing that, and come to her senses; and the worst thing that could happen was that Laura would fly to New York, and the seat beside her would be empty.

He shuddered, imagining Laura talking to the empty seat.

Mohammed took the unusual step of asking his father about Jehran.

"I do not want you involved with that family," said his father sharply.

Mohammed protested that he was not involved, just curious.

"That family is very questionable. If they are a family. I have doubts. I have sent you to an international school so you will better know the customs of the world," said his father. "You will go into business with me, and this knowledge will be helpful. But there are people with whom you will not associate."

This made Mohammed more curious. "What do you know about Jehran's family that—" His father simply looked at him, and Mohammed ceased to speak.

Mohammed was appalled by how American boys talked to their fathers. This was when he knew that he and they came from different worlds. When Mohammed's father closed a subject, it stayed closed.

But he knew his father's prejudices. He sorted through them, wondering which applied to Jehran's family. If they were a family. What could that mean?

Drugs were the strongest possibility. The family, or group of criminals, could be a conduit for drugs from Afghanistan or Iraq or Iran or Syria.

Extreme fundamentalist religion was not likely. If the family was rigid in its Islamic beliefs, Jehran would not be in a school attended by boys and Americans.

Violence was possible. If the family gave money to, say, extremists in Syria who put bombs on Israeli buses, Mohammed's father would never associate with them.

Mohammed did his schoolwork. He watched some television. During the evening news, it occurred to Mohammed that there was one violent act that had taken place near Jehran.

The murder of Billy Williams.

o   o   o

For Laura's parents to believe she was going to Edinburgh, she would have to get a permission slip from Mr. Hollober.

L.I.A. believed in detail. The permission slip would include the hotel in Edinburgh, its phone number, the names and phone numbers of chaperones, suggested clothing and spending money, instructions for meeting the return train.

Laura tried to believe that her mother and father would not call her up in Edinburgh to see if she was having fun.

After class, Jimmy Hopkins got his permission slip. "Jimmy, this is great!" said Mr. Hollober. "I'm so glad you're coming. Your parents can sign this and fax it."

Laura took Jehran's arm and walked out of the room. In the hallway, she said, "Jehran, my mother will help me pack, she'll drive me to the station, she'll stay on the platform to wave good-bye. Mr. Hollober is sure to mention that I didn't pay for it and he isn't expecting me."

"Laura, don't be frantic. This will work. Now, distract Jimmy."

Laura did not know how to distract Jimmy Hopkins. Or anybody else. And even if she did distract Jimmy, he would just be distracted and still holding his permission slip.

Jimmy came out of Mr. Hollober's room slowly, because he had such an armload of books, and he was trying to slide the permission slip into his notebook without bothering to open the notebook.

Jehran said, "Jimmy, may I borrow your notes? I want to photocopy them. I drifted off during the lecture."

"He didn't say anything important," said Jimmy, not handing her his notebook.

"Jehran likes unimportant details," said Laura. "She's the kind who studies during vacation. Let her have them, Jimmy."

Jimmy laughed. "Okay, Jehran. All two lines of notes. They're yours." He handed over the notebook. His permission slip lay crookedly inside the cover.

"Whoa-eeee!" shouted the Americans when school was over. "Not only is the sky blue—the sun is shining!" In London, this was to celebrate.

A softball game began on one of the school diamonds. Laura got that dizzy time-slip feeling when she couldn't quite tell if she were in Boston or London. Baseball made her happy, though. She loved the sound of ball against bat.

Mohammed stood next to Laura. She wanted to say, *So Mohammed, if you were a teenage Moslem girl, and your family was marrying you to the man they chose, and you hated him, and you ran away—what would they do to you if they caught you?*

Actually, from Mr. Hollober's class and Samira, she knew the answer: you wouldn't run away. You would be delighted that your parents had chosen a sensible nice man from a good family.

And Mohammed wasn't dumb. He knew the only Moslem girl with whom Laura was friends was Jehran.

So she could not ask Mohammed anything.

She wanted advice.

But there was nobody to ask.

"I gave up understanding Thanksgiving," said Mohammed, "but that's history. Now we approach Christmas. Tell me about Christmas."

She knew he didn't mean religious Christmas: any Moslem understood sacred days. He meant American Christmas. The month of December.

At Christmas, people were leaving London. Many Americans were Going Home. This was said reverently, as if speaking of a shrine. But just as many were going to ski in Switzerland or safari in Kenya. Laura dreaded Christmas. How were the Williamses going to celebrate?

Samira joined Jehran on the far side of the diamond, and the two laughed in that Euro-smile way. Laura remembered how anti-American Samira and Jehran usually were in Mr. Hollober's class. How Jehran thought so poorly of American families.

But in the end, thought Laura, she knows we're the only place to go. If you need a sanctuary, it's us.

"Once," said Laura to Mohammed, because she could not talk of light and life and Christmas, "Mom and Dad and Billy and I went to the London Dungeon. They had some really good ways to kill people back then."

"*Good* ways to kill?" asked Mohammed.

"You know what I mean."

"No, I don't. I don't think there are good ways to kill. I think there are only good ways to live."

"Oh Mo, don't be so perfect."

The nickname popped out. Americans liked nicknames. The shortening of a name was a sort of gift. She wondered, since he bore a sacred name, if changing Mohammed to Mo was like having a son named Jesus and calling him Jeez.

"I mean," said Laura, "when I catch the person who killed Billy, I'm not going to settle for a jail cell. I want that person stoned or squashed to death, the way they show you at the Dungeon."

"Don't say that," said Mohammed. "I've seen a woman stoned and it isn't something you could do, Laura, or that you'd want to witness."

But he was wrong. Laura could do it easily to the man who had killed her brother.

"I didn't know Billy except by sight," said Mohammed, "but I admired him. I liked his energy. He wouldn't want you to be thinking of these things. Not at the time of your Christmas."

A minute ago she had wanted Mohammed's advice; now that Mohammed was giving her advice, she hated him.

"Laura," said Mohammed, almost fiercely, "be careful in your friendships. Don't be such an American."

She was furious with him. "What business is it of

yours?" she demanded. "And what's wrong with being such an American?"

He spread his hands between them to filter her anger. "There's nothing wrong with being an American. But you lack suspicion."

"What are you talking about, Mohammed? All I do now is suspect people! I spend all day and night making lists! Lists of people who thought Billy was unsupervised! Lists of people who thought Billy was a nuisance! Lists of people who might know how to make bombs! I suspect sixth graders who bought Ritz crackers from Billy. I suspect neighbors, Mohammed. I suspect teachers. I suspect *you.*"

Con Vikary watched her former best friend stomp away, having yelled at the last person willing to cool her off.

Mohammed was expressionless, which Middle Eastern kids did very well.

Con felt cut up inside, as if Laura had yelled at her, instead of at Mohammed.

Laura got on a 113, Eddie having left the school before the ball game started. The bus pulled away from the curb before the last passenger was fully on. It seemed to rocket away from L.I.A.

Con had a sense of time running out, of a clock ticking, of an ending rushing toward her.

But other things ticked besides clocks.

Bombs ticked.

CHAPTER
13

Laura Williams stood in her own flat and tried to talk herself into stealing her own brother's passport.

It isn't stealing. It belongs to us.

Daddy has never forbidden me to go into his desk.

But it was stealing. It didn't belong to Jehran. Although Daddy had never expressly said *Don't open that drawer*—it was certainly understood that his desk was not for his children to paw through.

Child, Laura reminded herself. He doesn't have children anymore. He has a child.

At night her parents tucked themselves into the envelope of each other. They went to bed together, safe under the same covers, while Laura was alone. She could not summon Billy. He had fully departed.

She was the only child.

She opened the drawer casually and pressed the bulging files together. At the back lay a zippered leather envelope. The passports were wrapped in a fat rubber band wound around twice. When that rubber band had been spread to go around the passports, Billy had been alive.

She took the rubber band off. She separated the passports. On the front of each tiny book was a golden eagle, USA, and a perforated passport number, but on the outside, no name and no photograph. On the outside, a passport was anonymous.

She opened the first.

It was Nicole's. Not new. Nicole had her old haircut and a shirt she didn't wear anymore.

Laura shuffled it to the bottom of the pack and opened the next.

Hers. Yucky, yucky hair, she looked as if she had the IQ of Cool Whip.

She kept it.

And the third was William Wardlaw Williams.

He was so little! He was so young.

Oh God! So young and so little and so dead.

Laura had to open her father's, to reassure herself that Thomas Williams was still himself. And he was. She put Nicole's and Thomas's back.

Billy, she told his picture, *I'll have a son someday. I can't name him William Wardlaw Williams, because I'll be married and I'll have a different last name. But I'll name him William.*

And she knew that she would not: there could never be another Billy.

o   o   o

Somehow Nicole figured out how to cook something and even put it on the table.

Life goes on, she reminded herself, but she did not want it to go on. She caught herself taking a strange, high step across the dining room floor, as if she thought she could step back to when Billy was alive.

She had signed the permission slip to go to Edinburgh.

It was sensible. Laura needed to put her life together. But Nicole could barely stand the thought of life coming together, closing without a gap where there ought to be Billy.

Thomas sat in front of the television, watching a British quiz show. It was the sort where there would suddenly be gales of laughter from the audience and no American viewer would know why. Thomas could not answer a single question.

He was killing time.

Or time was killing him.

December twenty-third was the last half day of school, and classes were thin. Many kids had already left. L.I.A. parents never thought the school calendar meant them. Nobody did any real work. The girls giggled and gossiped while the boys talked about American college basketball.

Laura had gotten excellent at talking softly. "Jehran, what about money? You have to live on something. New York is expensive."

"I will have ten thousand dollars in my carry-on," said Jehran.

Ten thousand dollars!

What if somebody went through her luggage and found so much cash? They often opened your bags at luggage checks; that was the point of luggage checks. And whether or not it was against the law to move that much money from country to country, it was certainly odd for an eleven-year-old boy. If the money were found, Laura and Jehran would be questioned, and then would come a phone call to her parents.

"As for living expenses," said Jehran, "I have removed money from my Swiss bank account and wired it to a new account in New York."

Laura's jaw dropped.

"In Billy's name," added Jehran.

Would Billy ever love that! Laura hoped it was a million dollars. A million dollars in Billy's name, straight out of an unnumbered account in Switzerland.

"At the airport," Jehran said, "you'll call me Billy, and I'll behave like your little brother."

As if the elegant Jehran could ever behave like Billy Williams. Laura said nervously, "Jehran, is Mr. Hollober right? What will your brother really do to you if we get caught?"

"It is in Allah's hands," said Jehran calmly. "If Allah wills my safe passage, I shall have it. If Allah does not, I shall not."

Laura was pretty sure Allah would expect Jehran to obey her brother. That's what Moslem women did: they obeyed the men in their family. So if it was in Allah's hands, Laura didn't see how it was going to work.

It's in my hands, thought Laura. But should it be?

Jimmy Hopkins woke up in the middle of the night.

It was a horrible awakening: that knife-in-the-heart kind, shakes and sweat from a bad dream.

He was dreaming of Billy's empty plane seat.

The bedroom was cold. English rooms were always cold. But this time, Jimmy's insides were cold, too.

He pulled his dream back. He couldn't always, because waking up shattered the dream, but this time he was able to reach inside and find the edges of his nightmare.

He had dreamed that somebody really was sitting in Billy's airplane seat.

Rentals in London were furnished. The Williamses' flat had come with furniture and sheets and television, vases for flowers, and a pencil sharpener. It even came with a maid two mornings a week.

But the flat did not come with Christmas ornaments. The very best were left at Grandma's: the spun-gold stars, the crystal angels. But Nicole had shipped strings of wooden cranberries, an evergreen forest of candles, and a manger with stacks of sheep.

And, of course, four stockings.

Nicole had gone through a cross-stitch stage the year Billy was born, embroidering four glorious stockings with kings and stars and sweet new babies on hay.

Filling stockings was a family activity. The Williamses had never gotten into the Santa Claus thing. Even when they were toddlers, neither Billy nor Laura expected a Santa. *They* were Santa. Each Williams was on the look out for things that were small and just right. Secret purchases were year-round.

Laura had found stocking presents for Billy ages ago: a miniature license plate with the name of their Underground Line, the Jubilee; a savings bank shaped like an old-fashioned red London phone booth; a collection of foreign change: Israeli shekels, Norwegian kroner, Italian lire.

She knew what Billy had gotten for her, too, because Billy was always so excited by his brilliant purchase, he'd have to get up in the night and show her.

On Christmas Eve, the Williamses went to church. Laura felt as if she were watching rituals performed by aliens from particularly strange planets. "How are we supposed to rejoice over this little boy being born when our little boy died?"

"The point is Easter, not Christmas," said her mother. "Jesus rose from the dead. And Billy, too."

Laura wanted so desperately to believe Billy still existed that the idea reversed itself and became idiocy. Quadrillions of people had died over the ages. Was there really some acreage where those souls hung out?

Anyway, she wanted to know what good it was to have your brother get eternal life if he got it somewhere else?

They drove home in silence. They trekked upstairs. Inside the flat, Nicole's attempts at Christmas decorating seemed obscene.

Laura gasped, shocked.

From the mantel hung four stockings. All four bulged.

At the wrong time, in the wrong place, had Santa suddenly shown up?

"I wanted to use Billy's stocking, too," said Nicole. Her words came out in jerks and pieces. "I found your stocking pile, Laura, and I found his, and I divided them up the way it looked right." She began to cry. "But it doesn't look right."

No. It didn't look right.

Nobody wanted to be in the same room with the stockings, and Laura knew that she wouldn't touch her stocking in the morning either.

Thomas stacked Christmas CDs to play all night long, and all night long, Laura listened to harps plucking and choirs singing and organs playing.

"So, God?" said Laura around two in the morning. She'd listened to so many carols about His baby being born, she felt He must be here. "So how come you're such a meanie?"

Her father heard her yelling at God. He came and sat on the edge of her bed. He looked young in pajamas, his thinning hair sticking up. "God wasn't a meanie, Laura. The terrorist was."

"But Daddy, why didn't God stop him?"

"Only other people can stop evil people."

"But we didn't know evil was coming. How were we supposed to stop it?"

"I don't know, sweetie. I guess . . ." He struggled with it. Laura hated to see her father struggle, as if he too were young and without answers. "I guess our job, as good people, is to try to stop evil where we do see it."

And was it evil for different countries to have different customs? Was it evil for Laura to interfere in Jehran's family decisions? Would it be evil if she did not?

On so many Christmas Eves, neither Laura nor Billy could fall asleep. The excitement of unknown gifts! The tension of waiting, and hoping hoping hoping to get wonderful, amazing things.

Now she was old and crushed, and who cared what was under the tree?

At three in the morning, hearing her parents mumbling, Laura got up. The carpeting padded her bare feet. She moved toward their closed door.

"I don't want her to go on this Edinburgh trip," said her mother.

Laura ceased to move.

"Nicky," said Laura's father, "she needs a breather. She needs to be a regular teenage girl for a few days, instead of a professional mourner. She needs to be away from us touching Billy's things and staring at Billy's empty chair. She needs some sort of Christmas. Some sort of celebration. I guess Edinburgh is it."

Laura could hear the irregular breathing of people trying not to cry. People who had cried enough and were teaching themselves to un-cry.

"But what if something happens to Laura?" Her mother's voice was a weeping heart.

"Nothing will happen."

"Thomas, I can't stand it! I could not live through it! *I cannot lose my other child.*"

Laura slid back to her room.

Don't take this one, too! Nicole was crying to a Fate that put her son in the wrong place at the wrong time.

Laura had been looking through broken glass. Now she saw the whole. Her mother and father needed her.

I will give Jehran Billy's final gift, Laura Williams decided, and then I will tell Mom and Dad that it's time to go home, whether they think so or not. They'll give in to me, and once we're home, we'll heal.

They were were beautiful words.
Home.
Heal.
Billy would say, Go for it.
Go home, he'd say. I'm okay.

CHAPTER 14

Jehran was stunning in a scarlet wool ankle-length coat. Her black hair had been woven to the side, the single braid a thick and glossy rope. Black suede gloves with lacy cutouts covered her hands, and black suede boots trimmed in braid gave her another three inches of height. From her shoulder hung a smart leather carry-on, swollen with possessions. She quite literally looked like a million dollars.

"Where have you been?" hissed Laura. *"I've been waiting half an hour."*

"I'm so sorry," said Jehran, embracing Laura first on one cheek, then the other. In her most clipped British accent, she explained, "My brother was difficult. He not only drove me to St. Pancras himself, but wanted to come in and hand me over personally to Mr. Hollober."

That would have been fatal. They had, of course,

157

never handed in their permission slips. Mr. Hollober was not expecting them.

"However," said Jehran, "there was too much traffic, and the police wouldn't permit my brother to leave the car, so I bade him good-bye and hurried into the station by myself."

"Did anybody see you?" demanded Laura.

If anybody actually going to Edinburgh, like Con or Jimmy, had seen Jehran, they would have run over to say hi and want to know where she was going, looking so fantastic, and Con would have exclaimed over the carry-on—more lies; more time wasted.

Jehran shook her head. "I walked straight out the opposite door and came here."

London, whose train stations were numerous, had another train station right next door—Euston. Here Laura and Jehran would take a taxi to Heathrow Airport.

Laura tried to calm down. The first hurdle was over. The second hurdle was to change Jehran into Billy.

In the ladies' room (the British used no euphemism; it was simply "toilet"), the girls entered the same stall.

Laura had two bags: her plain blue canvas gym tote and a very large opaque plastic bag from a dress shop. Joanna, it said in curly letters. The Joanna bag originally contained beautiful sweaters Nicole had bought before she understood the exchange rate. After Nicole grasped how many dollars she'd actually spent, the sweaters horrified her.

Laura's mother had been almost chipper that morning. The nightmare of Christmas over, Nicole even managed a good-bye kiss and a smile. "You have a wonderful time," she said, and Laura had never loved her mother more: Nicole really wanting Laura to have a good time; really believing that Laura was going to hike the streets of Edinburgh, tour a castle, listen to a bagpipe.

Nothing can go wrong for me, Laura told herself. The only things that can go wrong would go wrong for Jehran.

Jehran dumped the contents in Laura's arms and then stuffed her red coat into the Joanna bag. Under such a coat you would expect a fine suit or beautiful dress. No. Jehran had loose, faded blue jeans rolled above her knees, and a faded Mickey Mouse grinned joyfully from a sagging T-shirt. Jehran yanked off her boots, jammed them into the bag, and rolled her jeans legs down. She put on a pair of Billy's sneakers, ruined by London puddles.

Laura took nail polish remover from the makeup kit in her gym bag, and they removed Jehran's layers of vermilion polish. The little stall stank of acetone. Jehran clipped her nails down to the quick, like a nail-biting kid.

Around them, toilets flushed and hands were washed, women rushing between commute and work.

Laura's fanny pack held three sets of plane tickets: hers and "Billy's" for this morning's flight, with the returns in seven days, as if they really were going to visit their grandmother; and Laura's real return ticket, for this evening. She had bought that at a much nicer agency, and nobody'd paid any attention to her. Next to the tickets were two passports. Laura opened them to check that she really had her own and she really had Billy's.

She did.

She also had her mother's kitchen shears.

"Are you sure?" said Laura. It took so long to grow hair! This was Jehran's glory. "Jehran, we could still back out."

"*Billy*," corrected Jehran in a sharp whisper. Jehran handed Laura her hair, holding the fat braid rigidly from the side of her head. "I'm ready," said Jehran, and the Euro-smile briefly crossed her lips: that I-know-more-than-you-do smile.

The braid was thick, and the scissors dull. Laura hacked at it. It felt as if she were amputating an arm. When the foot-long braid finally came off, Jehran held it aloft, the little smile hot with triumph. Without a glimmer of regret, she dropped her hair into the Joanna bag.

"Sit on the toilet rim," whispered Laura. Standing above Jehran, she tried her best to trim the stubble of Jehran's straight black hair. Then, she took out Billy's beloved Red Sox baseball cap.

Billy had been an ardent Red Sox fan. Sometimes Billy had lived in this cap for weeks at a stretch. Back home, he and Daddy went to Fenway Park and cheered for a team that Billy used to say was not going to get a pennant in his lifetime . . .

. . . and it hadn't.

What if Daddy needed this cap, to turn around and around in his hands, and remember his son by?

Jehran took the cap, not knowing its meaning (what non-American could ever know the meaning? Laura was overwhelmed by all that Jehran would have to learn; afraid for her, filled with admiration for her) and jammed it down over the raw-cut hair.

It worked.

There was nothing like a baseball cap for turning you into a disheveled little boy.

They waited for a moment until nobody was washing hands, left the stall, and stuffed the Joanna bag into the big trash container. Laura dropped the shears in, too, because they would set off metal detectors at the airport.

Jehran shrugged into Laura's old denim jacket and slung her magnificent leather bag over her shoulder.

"Nope," said Laura, almost grinning. "No eleven-year-old boy from Boston would have that kind of bag. We'll switch. I'll carry that, and you'll take my gym bag."

"No," said Jehran.

Con Vikary was really looking forward to Edinburgh. There were great kids going, Mr. Hollober was a decent chaperone, and Con loved trains to the point of embarrassment. When she was little, she had wanted to be a train engineer, and sometimes when her parents talked of her future college and her long-planned spectacular career, she wanted nothing more than to yank the cord on a train whistle.

And to leave on a romantic journey from St. Pancras, the finest train station in the world! It was an extravagant brick creation, Disney castles done in red.

Con said uneasily to Mohammed, "I can't stop thinking about Laura."

"None of us can stop thinking about Laura."

"She asked me a ton of questions about Kennedy Airport," said Con. "As if she has to know her way around. The Williamses aren't going home for Christmas, and if they did go home, they'd fly into Boston."

Mohammed had no idea.

Con said, "I have this sick feeling about Laura. I just feel as if she and Jehran are up to something, and it isn't a slumber party menu."

"You're just jealous because she's better friends with Jehran now than she is with you," said Tiffany.

The conductor motioned to the L.I.A. group. He was smiling. It was time to board. Tiffany elbowed to be first.

"I'm not jealous," said Con. "I'm—I know this is excessive—but I'm scared."

"Call her up," said Mohammed. "Check on her

before we get on the train. Otherwise, your trip will be damaged with unfounded fears."

Laura loved British taxis. They were slumped over, like the rounded spines of old ladies. Inside, there was lots of leg and suitcase room, and the seats were hard and thin and foreign. She felt the same.

The drive to Heathrow seemed eternal. Was there any city on earth whose airport was within reasonable distance of downtown? Probably not.

Laura had flown only out of Logan, in Boston. Andrew and Con had worldwide airport knowledge, so Laura had asked them what Kennedy was like. Con thought it was the world's most poorly arranged airport. Andrew said there were plenty of contenders for that honor. Con said Kennedy was a wreck of temporary walls, stairs, and blockades, none of which had the right sign.

I won't know any more about Kennedy than the nearest refugee, thought Laura. But I can read English, so I'll know what the signs say, even if they say the wrong thing. Thousands of people survive Kennedy every hour. If they can do it, I can do it.

She patted her blue canvas bag. Inside she had traditional travel goods: paperback book—as if she could concentrate—crossword puzzles, new toothbrush, change of clothes.

Jehran hung on to her leather bag, totally ruining her look. Instead of being an anonymous eleven-year-old, she looked like an eleven-year-old who had just stolen a rich old lady's handbag.

"What do you think I'm going to do?" hissed Laura. "Steal your ten thousand dollars?"

There was lots of room between them and their driver, who was playing a gypsy radio station, and they talked beneath the music.

"I feel better holding it myself," Jehran said, keeping it on the far side of her body as if Laura might grab it.

"The police will think you snatched it." Once more Laura unzipped her fanny pack, checked the passports, fingered the tickets. Kissing her parents good-bye, she had known herself to be a traitor. The trust they placed in her! The worries they carried!

"Say hi to Edinburgh for me," her father had said, afraid to let go, and forcing himself.

What would her parents do if something went wrong?

Would they be scared to death?

"We're here," said Jehran in her most English accent. How could she pull off an American boy act when a sentence as short as that gave her away? Laura had to get Jehran to New York.

Laura paid the taxi driver.

Luggage carts were all over the place, like grocery

carts in American parking lots. Laura had worried over the baggage part. "It'll look funny if we don't have baggage," Laura said to Jehran. "We're supposed to be going for a week."

But Jehran could not pack much or her brother would have been suspicious.

Laura had considered bringing two real suitcases from home, one for herself, one for Jehran. They'd have to be full, because luggage got weighed; authorities would pause over two kids checking empty suitcases. But Laura had no way to get two suitcases out of the flat without her parents noticing.

If the duty officers questioned why Laura and Billy were traveling so light, Laura would say they were going to buy a whole new wardrobe while they were in America.

Laura was hurting at her joints, as if worry were arthritis. She shook her hands in the air to relieve the pain in her wrists.

Inside, Heathrow was jumbled and confusing. Laura struggled with signs that weren't there or contradicted each other. At last she found British Air.

"Plenty of time," she murmured to Jehran. "Hour and ten minutes before the flight leaves." She puffed out air in a hard little spout, as if she were preparing for a foul shot. "We're good to go."

A hot smile was on Jehran's mouth. For a moment, Laura had the odd, and unwelcome, feeling that Jehran was laughing at her. Don't be silly, thought Laura, it's her brother she's laughing at, and the old man she won't have to marry.

Carts jangled, children whined, metallic announcements blared.

They began the lengthy procedure of international flight.

Just to enter the passenger area, they and their luggage must pass through metal detectors.

Laura's hands were now cold as well as painful. Her spine was a rod of ice leaning on her back.

An Asian family—women in saris, children as dressed up as if they were going to a wedding, men wearing turbans—were talking to the official. He waved them through, and up went a man with a red and white kaffiyeh on his head like a knotted-up picnic tablecloth.

Directly in front of Laura and Jehran were two creepy men who might indeed be suspected of having dismantled submachine guns in their luggage. Their clothing was strange, their posture was odd, and their language sounded like ducks quacking.

"Did you pack this yourself?" said the officer.

The two men nodded.

"Did anybody ask you to carry something for them?" droned the officer.

The two men shook their heads.

Jehran switched the two bags, after all, taking Laura's navy canvas bag. It was Jehran's leather carry-on that Laura placed on the conveyor belt. "Did you pack this yourself?" said the officer. He hardly looked at her.

For a moment, Laura could not breathe. Then she said, "Yes."

"Did anybody ask you to carry something for them?"

Laura Williams was carrying an entire person. She was not smuggling drugs, or emeralds, or gold. She was smuggling a person.

But she said, "No."

Con Vikary stared into the railroad station phone as if there were a script written on it. "The Edinburgh trip?" she repeated.

"Yes. She left about an hour ago, Consuela," said Laura's father. "She'll be back late, day after tomorrow."

Con's pulse drummed inside her head. It made her ears hurt. "Okay. Um. Thanks." She could not think how to end the conversation with dead Billy's father. *Have a Happy New Year* did not sound likely. "Talk to you later, then, Mr. Williams," she managed. She continued to stare at the phone after she'd disconnected.

A German tourist behind her cleared his throat irritably. Con stumbled away.

Laura wasn't on the Edinburgh trip. Mr. Hollober didn't have her on the list. Nobody was expecting her. No hotel room and no roommate had been assigned to her.

Jimmy and Mohammed were signaling. The rest of the class group had boarded. The train wasn't leaving yet, but nobody liked standing on the platform; they liked finding their seats and settling in, getting cozy for the hours of staring out the window.

Con could not lift an arm to wave back. Laura had arranged two days away from home. She had lied to her parents. What for? Where was she? This had to be what she and Jehran were planning.

Con tried to think what friendship meant. Laura was sixteen and could make her own decisions, and if they were bad ones, she'd live with the results.

But bad decisions in the Williams family had once led to death.

Laura, if you had confided in me, I would have backed you up, thought Con. But she was not sure she would have, and not sure she could now.

Mohammed and Jimmy jogged over to her.

She was so afraid for Laura, and so mad at Laura, that she could not seem to speak, and all she could do was pluck at Mohammed's jacket.

The check-in counter had six clerks: women dressed in the fashion of airline personnel worldwide: crisp and tailored and somehow annoying.

A long queue of passengers curved back and forth, divided by ribbons on metal stands. People in line clutched tickets and examined passports yet again, reassuring themselves that the priceless little booklet was still there. Their passports were a different color from Laura's, and more booklike.

Laura had checked the tickets in her hand ten times to be sure she was handing over the right set, but she did not have the passports out. Americans were always faintly surprised to have to show identification, so Laura, too, must be surprised. She must frown a little and dig.

The line crept forward.

Passenger after passenger turned over plane tickets, and then passports, so a seat could be assigned and a boarding pass issued.

You have to be who you are, or you cannot get on a plane. You have to match the photograph in the passport.

When their turn came, Laura walked up to the counter without looking back to see if Jehran was being Billy.

The clerk had the kind of fingernails Jehran had had a few hours ago: long and hard nails that tapped noisily on the computer keyboard. "You and—?" said the clerk.

"My brother," said Laura. "Aisle seats, please, but we don't have to be across from each other."

The clerk nodded, typing away, finding a seat combination. "Traveling without your parents?"

"We're going to our grandmother's for a week."

"Suitcases to check?"

"No."

The woman looked up at this. They always looked up at anything unusual. "Traveling light," she observed.

"We're going to buy new stuff once we're home," Laura explained. "Grandma lives near a great outlet mall. We'll come back with way too much luggage." Her smile felt like a strap across her teeth.

The clerk lost interest. "Passports, please."

Laura produced them.

The woman flipped through the passport pages slowly, as if expecting to learn something truly fascinating.

Laura looked at the little booklets upside down. The color of Billy's complexion, eyes, and hair were Jehran's. There seemed no resemblance beyond that. But their own mother had seen it. Would the airline personnel?

A kid's passport lasted five years, but kids change a lot in five years. A photograph that didn't quite match would not be unusual for a kid.

The clerk looked back and forth between the photograph of Billy and the person of Jehran. Laura's teeth got cold. Jehran turned the Red Sox cap in circles on her choppy hair, paying little attention to the clerk.

The woman handed back passports, tickets, and the precious boarding passes. "Boarding in thirty minutes."

"Thank you," said Laura Williams. "Come on, Billy."

CHAPTER 15

Jimmy was horrified by Con's face. Her mouth drooped as if she'd had a stroke. Her eyes were way too wide, as if her skin were splitting.

"I was on the phone," said Con, pointing, as if Jimmy and Mohammed had forgotten what phones were. "I was nervous, and I just felt like checking. Laura isn't home. Laura's told her parents that she's on this trip."

Jimmy's blood turned to glue. He felt himself slow down inside. That explained the plane tickets. What a horrible thing for Laura to do to her poor parents! Lying about something as huge as this, disappearing, when her mother and father had just had their only son disappear forever.

"I didn't tell. I just hung up," said Con. "I didn't know how to handle it."

Jimmy did not quite trust Mohammed and he didn't

quite trust Con and he didn't quite trust his own judgment.

But together, the three of them, classmates of Laura's, he trusted them as a group. "Listen to me. I've been so worried about Laura that when she was behaving exceptionally screwy last week, I followed her. She went to this sleazy travel agency and bought two round-trip flights to New York, *in her name and Billy's*. The plane leaves in an hour from Heathrow. She's lost her mind. She's planning to fly to New York with Billy's ghost."

Con and Mohammed stared at Jimmy. Con's face was coming back together, skin tightening along with her thoughts.

"I'm worried about her sanity," said Jimmy.

"Laura is not so crazy with grief," said Mohammed slowly, "that she believes Billy can fly to New York with her. She's bought that ticket for somebody else."

Jimmy had never thought of that. It was a hard thing to think of. What somebody else? How could there be a somebody else?

"*Somebody else?*" said Con. "But Mohammed, you have to travel with a passport that matches the name on the plane ticket."

"Yeah, Mohammed," said Jimmy, "you go through at least two—sometimes three or four—passport inspections."

"Then the person flying on Billy's passport looks like Billy," said Mohammed.

Jimmy could hardly follow this explanation. "You

mean Laura has lost her mind so completely, she's found a substitute for Billy? Some little kid she's taking to New York?" Jimmy felt his way toward some sort of understanding, but he didn't reach any.

Con shivered. "That's grotesque, Mohammed. You mean you think Laura is—like—*adopting* some little boy? Some little middle school kid to be Billy for her? But—but why? Who?"

"I don't think Laura's been in the middle school much," said Jimmy doubtfully, "where she could find a kid to substitute for Billy. She's been busy with her new friendship with—" Jimmy broke off. His image of Jehran, elegant in silk, faded to Jehran in her gym suit: skinny, boyish . . . Billy-ish.

"With Jehran," said Con.

Jimmy's mind was glue now. Each thought stuck to the next without making sense.

"I wonder," said Mohammed, "if Laura has managed to follow Billy's footsteps."

"You mean she really did figure out who Billy's killer is?" said Jimmy. "And this is some insane scheme to capture the killer by herself?"

"No," said Mohammed. "I am not fearful that Laura has found Billy's killer. I am fearful that Billy's killer has found Laura."

Airports were about lines.

About terrorists.

About fear.

Now came the second set of metal detectors, passengers walking through one, carry-on luggage going separately through another, and then they would be able to approach the gates.

Laura thought of the doomed Lockerbie flight, also a Christmas flight. It had been blown up over Scotland, throwing wreckage across eight hundred square miles. Every passenger on Pan Am Flight 103 and every carry-on had gone through metal detectors, but the bomb had been in baggage. Terrorists had checked a suitcase that contained a plastic explosive: semtex.

Ahead of them, person after person was setting off the alarm. In America, they used a handheld wand to run up and down your body in order to locate the keys or belt buckle or whatever had set off the detectors.

In England, they patted you down. They were serious about it. They frisked every inch, armpit to ankles.

Laura went through the detector first, and did not set off an alarm. Jehran followed, and did not set off an alarm.

Laura was so relieved, her legs were weak, as if she'd run for miles.

Their two bags moved slowly toward them on the conveyor belt for carry-ons. Jehran took back her leather bag, stroking its bulging sides, reassuring herself. Laura was also reassured. If there had been anything wrong, the man watching the X ray of each bag would have stopped them.

Jehran looked gender-free. Strangers would try to guess: pretty boy or crudely dressed girl?

Jehran was not looking at Laura. She was looking through the crowd: nervous parents keeping track of exhausted children; terrified foreigners with no idea what to do next; frequent flyers faded with boredom; flight attendants with their sharp high heels stabbing the floor as they strode to their gates, dragging their little suitcases on wheels like pets on leashes.

Jehran was not looking to see if anybody was following her. Jehran was not scanning the crowd for a hidden threat. She was neither afraid nor relieved.

Jehran was amused.

What is funny about people caught in exhaustion and worry? thought Laura. Why am I more afraid than she is? She should be terrified, because what if her brother parked his car and went into St. Pancras and checked with Mr. Hollober, what if even now he and his men are guessing where Jehran is? Talking their way past the inspectors?

Jehran caught the bill of Billy's Red Sox cap and pulled it down over her brow to hide her expression.

Americans might laugh over nothing. They got silly easily, and in public, too. But Jehran was completely not American. She wouldn't laugh over nothing. So she was laughing over something.

Like what? thought Laura. We aren't through the worst yet. We haven't gone through Passport Control.

They entered the upstairs limbo: duty-free shopping. A floor on which to kill time. The world *kill* filled Laura's brain. She swept it out. "Burger King," she said, pointing to a welcome sign. "We'll get Whoppers. No telling how long we'll be airborne before they get around to serving a meal."

Jehran was scornful. "I don't eat hamburgers."

"Billy, you adore hamburgers. You're an American. Burger, fries, and shake is your motto."

Jehran shook her head, insulted.

She's not refusing hamburgers, thought Laura. She's refusing to be an American.

It was such a shock to understand, Laura was physically jolted; thrown backward. I was right the first time, she thought. Jehran is completely not American. In fact, Jehran is anti-American. She's always been anti-American. So why does she want to go to New York? Where did she get ten thousand dollars in cash? Dollars, not pounds. What kind of family would have that much cash lying around in foreign currency? Money a teenager could pick up and take, without being noticed? Why would a younger sister inherit anything at all, when there's an older brother alive to inherit?

Why did Daddy think he was talking to Jehran's father, when Jehran's father is dead?

Why is Jehran in school if her family doesn't care whether a girl gets an education? If they hate Americans, why a school where fifty percent of the students are American? Why did they let her have a slumber party and invite Western girls?

Laura was seeing spots. Flashes like distant cameras broke in her eyes.

Jehran wrapped herself around Laura in a very feminine way, not at all like a little brother. "I'm so sorry, Laura. I'm scared. Please forgive me for being rude."

The apology was fake. Laura was a long-term expert on somebody—namely, the real Billy—apologizing without meaning it.

"I have never been anyplace in my life without an escort," said Jehran. "I have never done one single thing alone. All by myself I must learn America, from the moment you leave me in Kennedy Airport. I am so terrified."

But she was not terrified. Jehran was calmer than Laura, and at the back of her eyes, amusement remained. "I promise to learn to like hamburgers, Laura," she said.

On an international flight, you had to fill out a landing card: you had to write in your name, address, and occupation. Laura's father had a theory that nobody ever checked these, and he enjoyed giving himself unusual occupations. Pickle Taster. Global-Warming Manufacturer. No angry immigration official had ever arrested him for illegal filling-out-of-forms, so apparently he was right. Nobody checked.

What would Jehran's occupation be?

Laura fought with a word whose cruel letters wedged into her mind.

Terrorist?

Laura's head puffed. If she were to look in a mirror she would see a big white beach ball in place of her usual head.

Bombs and weapons could be made of plastic, not metal. Detectors depended on metal, but terrorists could not be depended on to use metal.

"Time to go to the gate," said Jehran. "Oh Laura, Heathrow is so frightening. I am so very, very grateful that you will be with me at Kennedy. How would I navigate without you?"

Up a wide, purple-carpeted ramp they went. A large sign read, Passengers Only. Laura's worry-thritis was now attacking her hips and knees and ankles. At this rate, she'd have to crawl on the plane.

In front of them was Passport Control.

Uniformed men and women practically lined the walls.

What would I say to them, thought Laura, if I said something? I know I am wrong. I must be wrong. *I want to be wrong.*

Laura looked longingly at those uniforms. She wanted them to stop her; she wanted them to make this decision. She would look foolish if she were wrong, and it would hurt Jehran's feelings, and everything would be ruined—they'd be caught—Laura would have to admit to her parents the depth and breadth of her lies—Jehran would be returned to her brother—

Jehran pressed against Laura as if she really were a little brother, afraid of getting separated. Billy had never worried about getting separated; the rest of the family had had to work to hang on to him.

We failed, thought Laura. We didn't hang on to Billy.

Who am I failing now?

Jehran?

My parents?

Or my fellow travelers?

"So what have we decided here?" said Con. Her brain was swerving like a test car among orange cones.

"We agree there is a resemblance between Billy and Jehran," said Mohammed, "and we have felt for weeks that Jehran is using Laura."

"But we don't know that there's anything actually dangerous or wrong," said Con.

"Why would Jehran want to get on an international flight without using her real name," said Mohammed, "unless she's going to do something she doesn't want discovered."

"Like what? What are you thinking of, Mohammed?" cried Con. "My thoughts aren't going wherever yours are going."

"Bombs," said Mohammed, "have been close to Laura before, have they not?"

Yes, of course. Bombs had killed her brother. But—

"So bombs come to mind," said Mohammed.

Bombs.

On a plane going home after Christmas.

Con was horror-struck. She actually felt slapped. Her face hurt. But she could not tolerate Mohammed's suggestion. "Come on. You're leaping from nothing to everything, Mohammed. Laura flips out, and you decide Jehran is—is—" Con could not say the sentence out loud: *Jehran is putting a bomb on a plane?* No.

"It doesn't feel logical," Con argued. Her voice felt strangled. Her throat hurt. "It isn't enough."

Mohammed shrugged. "Why should it be enough? Why should it be logical? Was there logic in your own Oklahoma, when a man bombed a day-care center?"

When Jimmy spoke, his voice had a gasping quality, like somebody choking on food. "Are you implying that Jehran killed Billy, Mohammed? I can't believe that! Why would she do that?"

"Perhaps she wanted this passport I think she is using."

"A passport," said Con, "is a piece of paper!" She tried to throw away Mohammed's silly talk. "Jehran wouldn't kill a little kid just for a piece of paper, would she? Jehran knew Billy. She couldn't pick out a kid she knew, could she? That's evil!"

Mohammed said patiently, "Terrorists are evil. Terrorism is evil. Evil is what Laura has been hunting for, and that, I believe, is what she has found."

What had Mohammed's life been, that he could come to such a conclusion?

Mr. Hollober came up behind them. "I have everybody aboard except you three," he said fussily. "Now get on the train."

Nobody even looked at him.

"Jehran despises Americans," said Mohammed. Mohammed often thought the worst of people because in his experience, the worst happened. "Her genealogy is based on hating Americans. Her country, which she loves, even though it will not have her, considers America to be Satan. So why is Jehran suddenly best friends with the very American Laura Williams? Laura Williams, the most naive of the naive."

"Why would Laura let Jehran use her, though?" As much as Con wanted explanations, she did not want Jehran to be the explanation. Strangers could be evil, but a girl who invited you to her slumber party, whose food you ate, whose books you borrowed, whose pencil you used—this person could not be evil.

"Maybe it's that Wild West image you cherish. Jehran spins a tale, and Laura wants to believe. Americans are easy targets."

"You don't have to be anti-American about it, Mohammed."

"I'm not, Con," he protested. "I love that about Americans. It's touching to go to school with Americans who really believe that deep down, everybody is good."

Con Vikary had become best friends with Laura on the first field trip of the school year. They'd gone to the medieval city of York, which was surrounded by a moat. The guide had explained that the moat had never been filled with water. It was a flaming moat. You filled the ditch with dry branches from the forest and set them afire to keep attackers from getting in.

"How would that work?" Laura had said, being difficult. Americans were always being difficult, and the Williams children were better at it than most. "I mean, what if it rained and the twigs got wet? And it's England, so it would rain. The bad guys would stroll into the city while the locals were still trying to light a fire."

Con could hardly wait to be best friends. She had invited Laura to sleep over, and they'd stayed up giggling and talking about boys, and now they could both face the school year eagerly: they had a best friend.

Billy was dead.

He would never again be difficult, or happy, or anybody's best friend, or talk about girls.

Sorrow filled Con's entire body: grief so huge, it did not fit.

Deep down, not everybody was good. Was Laura

going to run out of time to learn that? Could Mohammed possibly be correct? Was a bomb, once more,
close to Laura?

Mr. Hollober was not interrupting. Not con-
tributing. Just standing there, gaping at them.

Con Vikary was shaking. Not trembling. Shaking.
Her teeth had begun to chatter. If Mohammed was
right, the plane must be stopped. But Mohammed
couldn't be right, could he? They didn't even know
that Jehran was with Laura! This was all a string of
bizarre guesses. I went to a slumber party at Jehran's
house! thought Con. She can't be a—Con still could
not use the word "terrorist." What if we act on this?
she thought. What if we're wrong? What if we go and
do something that shuts down the airport for London,
England, and we're wrong?

Laura will be so mad at me! My father will go crazy!
The whole country will be so mad at me!

But what if Mohammed is right?

There was no time to gather actual facts. The plane
was probably boarding.

Con's shakes vanished.

"I have Mr. Evans's phone number," she said, and
ran back to the rank of telephone booths.

The Passport Control man was exhausted and bored.
Definitely not in love with his job or his fellow man.
"Traveling alone?" he snapped at Laura.

183

Laura nodded.

"You and your brother?" said the man.

Laura nodded.

How quickly the man flipped pages. How easily he waved them through and beckoned to the next person in line.

And that was that.

They would show their passports and tickets to get into the actual gate waiting room, but it wouldn't be a serious check. Just procedure.

They were home free.

Laura had an American dream: kids on the block back home playing hide-and-seek, kids under her maple tree, kids making it safely to base, shouting, *Home free!*

A thought blazed through Laura like a fire in the fireplace: welcome and sparkling. I'll turn around here. I won't go to New York, I'll go home.

Yet another long, wide, carpeted hall lay before them. Fellow passengers hiked on to the gate, dragging carry-ons, children, garment bags, briefcases, and computers. Laura Williams stopped walking.

The risk of terrifying her mother and father, of having them find out she was not in Edinburgh, was too great. She couldn't do it to them. And she didn't have to.

Jehran had not set off any metal detectors, so the horrible thought that had blindsided Laura could be set aside. "Jehran," she said softly, "I'm turning around here."

"*What?*" The huge soft eyes narrowed and hardened.

"You don't need me. You can manage the rest yourself."

"I do need you! If you don't make the flight, they won't let me on."

Laura shook her head. "Nobody cares if a passenger doesn't make the flight. That's their problem. But my problem is, my parents would be scared to death. It was necessary for me to give you the passport, but it's not necessary for me to come."

"*No!*" said Jehran, in a whisper that screamed. "Laura, you have to come! I didn't go through all these weeks of planning so that you could back out now!"

The racket and chaos of the airport filled Laura's brain and heart. They had not been planning this escape for weeks. The thing that had happened weeks ago, the thing that would have required planning, was Billy's death.

"*Weeks* of planning?" said Laura slowly.

Nobody had found a reason for Billy to die.

So many people had puzzled over that: *why choose Billy?*

If there were weeks of planning ... then Jehran had not thought of using Billy's passport after Billy's death. *Had she thought of using Billy's passport before Billy died?*

185

"Oh Jehran!" whispered Laura. It was not a whisper for keeping a secret, but a whisper because her lungs had leaked, like yesterday's balloon.

Laura remembered what she had wanted to do to Billy's killer: good ways to die.

The single thing Laura Williams wanted was to take Billy's Red Sox cap back and walk away.

She could not stand next to, or think about, or touch, a person who would take a child's life in exchange for a piece of paper.

"You didn't kill him yourself, did you?" said Laura dully. "You had it done. Those men in your house— maybe even the man you pretend is your brother—they did it, didn't they?"

Jehran did not agree—but she did not disagree.

A normal, nice person would be shocked, *horrified*, to be accused of murder.

Jehran was not, therefore, a normal, nice person.

I went looking for Billy's killer, thought Laura, and I found her.

If Jehran was responsible for Billy's death, then she had figured out how to escape using Billy as well. For what had Laura agreed to do? She had agreed to smuggle Jehran out of the country. No wonder Jehran was amused. Laura was not catching her brother's killer: she was rescuing her brother's killer.

Jehran touched the zipper of the elegant swollen leather satchel of which she had been so protective. She traced its tiny railroad tracks with the pad of her finger. She smiled her hot secret smile. "Now, Laura," said Jehran, "I need you, and you don't want to die the way Billy did."

CHAPTER 16

Laura yanked the leather case from Jehran's hands. She used all the strength she possessed, thinking Jehran would have a serious grip on something so important to her, but Jehran had not dreamed Laura would have enough guts to seize it and was holding it loosely. Laura staggered backward, possessor of the leather bag.

Jehran tried to get it back, but Laura kicked her against the wall and this, too, was effortless because Jehran never dreamed that Laura would actually fight.

"You don't have a bomb in here," said Laura scornfully. "You have money. If you had a bomb, you wouldn't be fighting to get this back in your own hands. You'd be laughing yourself sick because I'm the one hugging the bomb. Just like my brother."

Jehran, whom she had thought so beautiful and exotic. Only her selfishness was extraordinary. The extraordinary ego of evil.

"You don't have a Cause, Jehran," said Laura. "Your Cause is yourself." Laura had thought she would rip Jehran to pieces, but one kick was enough. Finding Billy's killer was good—but Billy was not back. Laura was sobbing, her voice was choked and broken with despair. "When I cut your hair, and you said 'I'm ready,' you didn't mean that you were ready to die, Jehran. You were ready to have a new life. You are not ready to blow up a plane you're about to board."

No passenger was too tired to miss this sentence.

People stopped walking.

People began backing away.

"You murdered my brother, Jehran," said Laura Williams. "And all for a piece of paper with a photograph on it, so you could become a New Yorker, while Billy became dust."

People screamed, ran, or dropped to the floor. They tried to find exits where there were only flat walls. They hid their children behind their backs. They protected their faces with their laptops.

Jehran knew when to give up and start Plan B. She simply turned and walked away. In the midst of this terrified crowd, she would be just another little kid in a jeans jacket. Airport security assumed you wouldn't dare race past them. Jehran, however, would dare anything. She'd run through Passport Control, vanish in the crowds, dart among the luggage carts and the endless lines. She would not get to America . . . but she would get away.

Laura was about to set the carry-ons down, to run after Jehran, when she knew what Billy had known, in his final terrible moment. If Laura's guess was wrong— if Jehran's intent was an explosion, if Laura did hold a bomb in her arms—did it matter whether they were on the plane?

She, Laura, could not do less than Billy. Whether the case contained money or a bomb, Laura Williams could not set it down.

The crowd changed color.

Laura could not figure out what was happening, why hundreds of people suddenly looked alike and went from wall to wall, all the way across, like a row of soldiers.

Well—because they were soldiers. Airport security, anyway.

Dozens of stiff people gripped Jehran, and dozens more surrounded Laura. "Miss Williams?" They were stiff, she realized, from fear. "Please don't open the bags. Just stand very still."

People were asked to leave the area quickly and quietly.

Never were people more cooperative. In seconds, there was security, and there were two passengers: Laura and Jehran.

Laura was calm for the first time since Billy's death. Jehran was not getting away with murder after all. And if Laura did not have all the answers, at least she had some answers. There was not nothing. There was something.

"She had my brother slaughtered," said Laura. "Go to her house. It's full of soldiers, and I believe she paid one of them to put a bomb in my brother's hand."

"What are you talking about?" cried Jehran. She could make no gestures, because her hands were tightly held, but her beautiful face spoke for her. "I thought/you were my friend, Laura." How feminine she looked, in spite of the haircut and the lopsided Red Sox cap. How frail. How innocent.

And how clever, thought Laura.

Laura knew how it was done now—easily. You make friends first, and Laura was an easy friend to make. You chose a friend who didn't listen, didn't want warnings, couldn't add up clues.

Jehran had found a perfect set: the passport that resembled her and the friend who would fall for it.

A squadron of men took Jehran's leather carry-on and Laura's blue one. Then they walked the girls through a door marked Authorized Personnel Only and into a room crowded with people; crowded with anxiety and anger.

Laura thought: I did this. I can't blame this fear and trouble and canceled flight on Jehran. I was angry with Mr. Evans and Mr. Hollober and Con's father and Mohammed . . . as if being annoyed is a reason to keep secrets!

Billy was man enough to know what was happening and to die to save the people around him, but I was a child, and risked the people around me.

I was an accessory to evil.

How young and innocent Jehran looked between these guards. Incapable of throwing a baseball, never mind a bomb. Indeed, the people who surrounded both girls did not look convinced. They were giving Jehran the benefit of the doubt. They were about to let go of those slender wrists. Poor little thing.

Never had Laura been so glad to see a thin man in a large jacket. "Oh, Mr. Evans!" she cried. Nobody stopped her when she ran up to him.

Mr. Evans barely stopped himself from taking Laura's shoulders to shake the stupidity out of her. "You should have called me," he said, "when Jehran first asked for Billy's passport."

"How did you know she asked for anything?"

"Your overachieving school friends are not just sitting around doing calculus, Laura. They've been terribly worried about you. They even followed you and found out about the plane ticket you bought in Billy's name. But did they call me right away? No! *They* waited till the very last moment, too!"

192

"Who called?" said Laura.

"Con, Jimmy, and Mohammed."

I was so rude to them, thought Laura, and they stuck by me.

"Dear Mr. Evans," said Jehran, in her beautiful convincing British speech, "I, too, am so glad to see you. Please ask your people to let go of me. You are unnecessarily alarmed. There isn't a bomb, just money. I am faced with a sad personal problem, and Laura volunteered to help me leave the country. Laura came up with a brilliant plan. Laura wanted to do this to honor her brother."

Laura was outraged—and afraid. What if they believe her? thought Laura. I believed her. "No!" said Laura. "*You* killed Billy. But it wasn't necessary, Jehran! If you wanted Billy's passport, why not just come to my house and take it?"

And then, after so much time trying to see the truth, Laura guessed some of it. "Those men downstairs in your house," she breathed. "They are terrorists, aren't they? That is their occupation, isn't it?"

Jehran said nothing.

Laura felt her whole body flying apart, her rage demolishing her, as if she were stoning herself. "Were they going to kill some American, anyway, Jehran?" shouted Laura. "Is that why they sent you to school with Americans? Was it your job to find a target?"

Jehran said nothing.

"What a great terrorist statement," said Laura. *"We can kill any little American kid abroad if we feel like it."*

Finally Jehran spoke. "It is cruel and heartless of Laura to suggest that I had anything to do with Billy's death," she told Mr. Evans.

"They killed the person you picked," said Laura. "And you picked Billy, didn't you? Admit it, Jehran!"

Mr. Evans was holding Laura by the shoulders now, but she did not stop shouting. "Billy was a great pick. People *were* terrorized. Dozens of people fled London and jerked their kids out of schools or moved back home. And you would have gotten freedom in the bargain. From me! The sister of your own murder victim."

Jehran said coolly, "Like all Americans, you watch too much television and draw foolish ideas from it. You have no proof."

"Jehran," said Mr. Evans, "we investigated every student in that school who appeared to have a relationship with Billy or Laura Williams. I know where you live, and the unusual nature of your family. As soon as I called the airport to stop this flight and hold you, I had the Metropolitan Police go to the mansion. They called me on my car phone. Your house is empty. Whoever leased it is gone. They filled their suitcases and left."

Laura was stunned.

In fact, she thought Jehran was stunned. Jehran's

beautiful olive skin became blotchy, like a bruise. Jehran definitely had not expected this news. What *had* she expected?

Mr. Evans asked questions, but Jehran ceased speaking. She slumped down, appearing younger and shorter. Those were the defenses she had now: childhood and silence.

Perhaps Jehran would never talk. The killer in Oklahoma City hadn't. The terrorists of Pan Am 103 were never extradited from Libya, so they never talked.

Laura held the Red Sox cap. What would Billy have thought of the mess she'd made? "I'm sorry, Mr. Evans," she said. "I never made more dumb decisions all in a row."

Mr. Evans did not excuse Laura. He nodded, still angry. Perhaps he would always be angry. "I'm taking you home, Laura. Your parents will feel better once you're in the flat with them."

Laura was sick. "My parents know?"

"Yes. And if you think having a police officer pull your father's car off the road a *second* time was easy for him, think again. Your mother and your father have gone through enough. This time, put them first."

Laura and Mr. Evans walked back out of the airport. He flashed an ID, but they still went through metal detectors. They emerged on a sidewalk in surprisingly bright sunlight. Laura felt as if she had been inside a capsule, enclosed by death and evil.

"I was going to put my parents first, Mr. Evans. I wasn't going to get on the plane after all. The original plan had been to go to New York with Jehran, but—"

"The only good plan," said Mr. Evans, "is for your family to go home."

EPILOGUE

Jehran had had only money in her carry-on.

None of her relatives were located.

Nobody who had lived in the mansion surfaced.

There was no proof that they or Jehran had been involved with any terrorist act.

In England, as in America, proof was required.

In England, as in America, sometimes the guilty went free.

The girl called Jehran remained silent. She was judged to be a minor, and put in a foster home.

She walked away after a few months and was not found.

And the Williams family went home.

Home without Billy.

It was unthinkable, but they did it, anyway. Some

days, life was good because it was familiar and it was theirs. Other days, it was terrible because a little boy who loved life didn't have it anymore.

Laura's friends wrote. She heard from Con and Mohammed, she heard from Jimmy, she even heard from Tiffany.

Every winter for years, the Williams family had gone skiing in New Hampshire. There was no Billy, but there was still snow, and cold, and beauty, and the hard glorious work of skiing.

Coming down the slope, Laura would try to cast grief into the snow-laden wind.

But thoughts of Billy did not lie gently. Billy might rest in peace, but the world did not. Every senseless act of violence the world over made her heart burst for her brother. Laura would shout, "No!" into the wind, but nothing Laura ever said or did could bring a child back from death.

She knew only this: she had been loved. Not just by her brother, but by all the friends who cared enough to pay attention, to risk looking silly, to get involved. Laura must honor Billy with the same courage.

Good-bye, Billy! she would cry in her heart. We will always love you. We will never fill your place.